THE LADY IS DEAD

by

PATRICK LAING

Author of "A Brief Case of Murder,"
"The Shadow of Murder," *etc.*

The blind psychologist Patrick Laing is once again obliged to put his academic theories to practical use when the university where he teaches is rocked by the repercussions of an old scandal and the reverberations of Murder.

Over twenty years before, Helena Stedman had been a beautiful and popular actress, and many of the men now on the university faculty, including the dignified Dean Prentiss, had been more than half in love with her. Then had come a fall from grace, her retirement and death.

All of this seemed to have little to do with the scientist Eric Fordyce's disapproval of his son's theatrical ambitions; Fordyce's untimely demise in a fire in his laboratory apparently had a much closer connection with atomic bomb and other top Government secrets.

In fact, it took a blind man to see that art and science are sometimes not so far apart as they appear.

THE LADY IS DEAD

The Lady Is Dead

by

Patrick Laing

WILDSIDE PRESS

THE LADY IS DEAD

CHAPTER I

"Helena Stedman," Prentiss said, and there was a wistful, far-away note in his voice, as if he were remembering a vanished love, "was the most remarkable actress I have ever seen—and the most beautiful woman. I'll never forget the summer she gave a course of lectures here at the university dramatic school. All of the male students—and a large part of the faculty, I think—were more than half in love with her. But that was over twenty years ago." His words trailed away into silence, as if those intervening years had blown like a cold wind across his heart.

"And you were one of them, perhaps?" Barto asked. He was our new professor of applied dramatics, and hadn't been with us long enough to know that one didn't put personal questions of that sort to our slightly pompous dean, even in the informal surroundings of the Faculty Club.

"I suppose I was." Prentiss laughed depreciatingly and a little self-consciously. "I was a young English instructor then, in love with art and consequently in love with love."

"What eventually became of the lady?" I inquired. Her name, when he had first mentioned it, had sounded vaguely familiar to me.

"She died," he answered briefly.

"Wasn't there a scandal of some kind about her?" Van Zittar, one of my colleagues in the psychology department, pursued. "I was too young at the time she flourished in the theater to remember much about it, but I seem to recall something. . . ."

"There was," Prentiss admitted. "And it was all the more—er—spectacular because nothing even remotely suggestive of obliquity had ever been associated with the name of Helena Stedman before. She'd been married to a man not in the theatrical profession—a scientist of some kind, I believe, whose name I don't remember. The year after she gave her lecture course here, she went to Hollywood to make a picture. During the filming of it, she fell in love with her leading man, a foreign importation who was expected to take the place of the late Rudolph Valentino, and who might have succeeded in doing it if he and Stedman had never met. There followed the usual scandal, in this instance a trifle lurid even for Hollywood."

He paused, not for dramatic effect, but because, being Prentiss, he always seemed to feel a vague embarrassment at discussing matters of this nature, as though he suspected that they robbed him of some of his scholastic dignity.

"She was granted her divorce from her husband exactly one month after her baby was born," he finished stiffly.

Van Zittar, who upon occasion can be somewhat coarse in his reactions, gave a slightly vulgar whistle. "Wow!" he exclaimed. "If you mean what I think you mean—and I've no doubt that you do—I'll bet that set tongues a-wagging, even back in the Roaring Twenties. And after such an episode, I suppose— Are you leaving us, Barto?"

Antonio Barto had risen. "I'm afraid I must," he said apologetically. "I wish to prepare a written examination for my class in stage technique for tomorrow morning." He turned to me. "If you're leaving at this time too, Professor Laing," he said, "I shall be happy to have your company across campus."

I accepted his invitation, and we left the Faculty Club together.

But although he had requested my company, as we walked together through the cool stillness of the early spring night, he seemed lost in his own thoughts; and I received the impression that they concerned matters which were of more importance to him than the examination he had said he wanted to prepare for his class.

"I imagine," I remarked in order to make conversation after we had progressed for several minutes in silence, "the affair Dr. Prentiss was telling us about ended Miss Stedman's career as an actress."

Barto made a sound in his throat that was half disgust, half contempt. "There is no doubt that you are right," he answered in his precise English, which still retained a faint trace of a Spanish accent. "It was a great injustice to a great artist. You Americans!" He spat out the words as though they had been something bitter in his mouth. "You will never learn to appreciate art for itself alone, but you must go poking your clumsy fingers into that which does not concern you. Helena Stedman's private life was her own affair; she had a right to do with it as she chose."

Having some slight knowledge of the Latin attitude in such matters, I wasn't surprised by his outburst. "Theoretically I agree with you," I replied. "The art should not be judged by the private life of the artist. But unfortunately or otherwise, we Americans are so constituted that we demand a certain amount of conformity to the generally accepted standards of moral integrity in those we place upon our public pedestals. Otherwise, we cannot feel sure of their sincerity in anything."

"Conformity!" he exclaimed passionately, and I heard a pebble skip across the path, as though he had kicked at it viciously as he walked. "Always there must be conformity to standards set up by others! Yet you prate of individual liberty, of the individual's right to—"

He broke off with a self-conscious laugh. "Forgive me," he said more quietly. "I didn't mean to read you a lecture. It is only that we of the theater are inclined to speak with greater vehemence than we intend. It often creates the impression that we feel more strongly upon a subject than is actually the case."

Although my blindness prevented me from seeing his expression, I wasn't deceived by the apparent lightness with which he dismissed the subject. It was one which, I was positive, went deeper with him than he wanted me to suspect.

By this time we had reached the edge of the campus, where we said good night and went our separate ways. As I turned in at my own front walk a few minutes later, the faint, sweet scent of wood violets told me that my wife, Deirdre, was waiting for me on the porch.

"What was Dr. Prentiss holding forth on this evening that kept you so late, Paddy?" she greeted me. "The unspeakable imbecility of the Government in Washington or the intellectual poverty of present-day American literature as exemplified by the modern novel?"

I laughed, and sat down beside her on the swing. "Neither, Derry," I answered. "In some way—don't ask me how, for I haven't the faintest idea—the subject got around to an actress whom he'd admired in his youth; one who made a rather spectacular fall from grace, smashing both her own career and the Seventh Commandment in the process."

"Was that why Dr. Prentiss admired her?" Deirdre asked innocently. "Or shouldn't I ask?"

"You should know better than to ask," I told her, slipping my arm about her slender shoulders. "However, I believe the old fraud actually enjoyed repeating that piece of scandal about her, once he got started. Barto, our new dramatics man, was there, and I'm afraid he got a little disgusted with what he evidently considers our provincial American attitude toward artists and morality. On the way across campus, he started to give me a spirited lecture on the subject, then suddenly checked himself."

"He probably remembered just in time that he was talking to a psychologist," Deirdre observed shrewdly. She settled herself more comfortably in the crook of my arm; then with an abrupt change of subject, "By the way, Paddy, I almost forgot: Mark Fordyce came over to see you this evening. He seemed disappointed when I told him you weren't here."

"Did he want to see me about anything in particular, or was it just a social call?" I inquired. Young Mark Fordyce, in addition to being one of my best students in behavioristic psychology at the university, was the son of our next-door neighbor, Dr. Eric Fordyce, who had moved to our city a little over a year before to work with one of the men in our chemistry department on some experimental work which I suspected had Government backing. He was not, however, an actual member of our faculty.

"He told me," Deirdre replied in answer to my question, "that Professor Barto had offered him the leading role in the Senior play this year. I believe he wanted to talk it over with you."

"The Senior play! Mark!" I exclaimed. "And his father violently opposed to dramatics in any shape or form. Oh, good Lord!"

"I think that was what he wanted particularly to discuss with you," Deirdre said. "He knows that if he accepts the part, he'll have to tell his father about it sooner or later, and he probably wants you to advise him as to the best approach. Paddy, why do you suppose Dr. Fordyce is so very antagonistic to Mark's interest in the theater?"

"Heaven alone knows," I answered. "Unless it's that, being a serious-minded scientist himself, he can't bear the thought of a son of his going into a field which must appear frivolous to him by comparison."

"That could be the explanation, I guess," she agreed thoughtfully. "Dr. Fordyce is a strange man. At times he seems passionately devoted to his son, while at others he's so strict with him, it's almost as if he actually hated him."

She paused a moment, then added speculatively, "I wonder whether Professor Barto would have offered Mark the part in the play if he'd known about his father's attitude."

A little to my own surprise, I found myself speculating with something more than casual interest upon what Barto's attitude in the matter would have been. Although the man and I had become only casual acquaintances since his arrival on campus the preceding fall, there was that about him which piqued my curiosity. With his fiery Latin temperament and his own particular code of ethics, he was in many ways a wholly unpredictable **quantity.**

Deirdre broke across my thoughts with an apparently irrelevant question. "Paddy," she asked, "do you suppose Mark's mother could have been Irish?"

"Why?" I teased. "Because of his flair for dramatics?"

"Of course not," she answered. "Because of his coloring. Dr. Fordyce is blond, almost the Nordic type, but Mark has black hair and deep blue eyes, the same as you have."

"The combination of black hair and blue eyes isn't confined to Northern Ireland," I reminded her. "Mark could have inherited the one from his mother and the other from his father. Incidentally, he never knew his mother. He told me once that she died when he was born."

Deirdre's small, cool hand came to rest upon mine. "I wonder," she speculated, "whether that's why Dr. Fordyce acts at times as though he hated his son. If he loved his wife very much, he might blame Mark. . . ."

"For having been the cause of his mother's death?" I inquired. "I doubt it, Derry. Dr. Fordyce is too fair-minded a man for that sort of melodramatic injustice. However, it's a pity he can't be more in sympathy with the boy where this question of a theatrical career is concerned. In his way, Mark is as strong-willed as his father. I'm afraid there may be real trouble over this matter of the Senior play."

We sat for a little while in silence then, both thinking about the boy and his problems. Suddenly the stillness around us was ripped to pieces by the sound of a sharp explosion that seemed to have had its origin not more than a hundred feet from where we sat. We both sprang up from the swing.

"Merciful heaven," Deirdre exclaimed. "That came from Dr. Fordyce's garage, where he's set up his experimental laboratory! Come on, Paddy; we must go over there and find out whether he's been hurt."

CHAPTER II

With Deirdre's arm linked through mine to guide me, we hurried across the intervening stretch of lawn in the direction of the Fordyce property. As we reached it, a door at the rear of the house slammed, and Mark Fordyce shouted to us.

"Professor Laing, can you help me?" His voice was tight with fear that was verging on panic. "That explosion came from Dad's laboratory, and he's in there! Can you help me get him out in case—"

He didn't stop to finish the sentence, and I heard his running footsteps pounding down the drive ahead of us.

"Does the place appear to be on fire, Derry?" I asked as we hurried after him. "If it is, you'd better run back to the house and call the fire department."

"No," she answered. "I don't see any flames, and there's no smell of smoke—" She broke off and released her pent-up breath in a sigh of relief. "There's Dr. Fordyce now, standing in the doorway," she told me. "And he doesn't look as though he'd been hurt."

"It's all right, everybody," Eric Fordyce's quiet, almost coldly reserved voice called to us. "No damage has been done. At least no serious damage."

Mark had reached his father's side by that time. "Dad, what happened?" he demanded. Relief and a still lingering anxiety made his own voice not quite steady. "Are you sure you're not hurt?"

"Positive, Mark." There was a depth of genuine affection in Dr. Fordyce's voice as he spoke to the boy. "Gas formed in a test tube that I was heating over a Bunsen burner, and it exploded. Against the surrounding stillness of the night, it probably sounded a lot worse than it actually was. Which means I'll have to be more careful in future, or I'll find myself being regarded as a neighborhood nuisance, if not a downright menace." He gave a brief, half rueful laugh, which was evidently intended to dismiss the whole matter.

"There's a cut on your left cheek, Dr. Fordyce," Deirdre pointed out as we came up. "It's bleeding."

"Probably a scratch from a splinter of flying glass," he said negligently. "I'll put a bit of plaster on it as soon as I've cleaned up the mess in here. Sorry if I frightened you, my dear, with my extemporaneous fireworks—you, too, Laing. And now if you'll both please excuse me . . ." He went back into the laboratory, and I heard the door close behind him.

"Well, I'm glad it was no worse than that," I observed to Mark as Deirdre and I turned to go back to our own place; then, remembering my wife's statement that the boy had called to see me earlier that evening, I added lest he should think I didn't want to be bothered by him, "By the way, Mark, Derry tells me you had something you wanted to discuss with me."

"I did have, Professor Laing," he answered—still a little shakily, I noticed. "But after what just happened, or almost happened, I'm afraid I don't feel up to talking about it tonight. So if you don't mind, I'll let it go until some time tomorrow morning, when we've both got a free period."

I assured him that I didn't mind in the least. "I'll be in my office in the psychology department between ten and eleven," I said. "You can drop around then."

It was a few minutes after ten the following morning when he arrived at my office in College Hall. As Deirdre had suspected, the thing he wanted to talk to me about was the matter of his father and the Senior play.

"I don't know what I ought to do, Professor Laing," he said when he had told me all about it. "If I tell Dad now, he'll forbid my accepting the part at all. If I don't tell him and accept it without his knowledge, he'll find out eventually from some other source, and then there'll be one devil of a row. Either way, it looks as though I'm headed for trouble."

"If I were in your place, Mark," I told him, having already given the matter some thought before his arrival, "I'd tell him at once, and get it over with. If you don't, he'll blame you later not only for having done something which you knew would be contrary to his wishes, but for having been secretive about it as well. Besides, there's always the chance that you may be able to overcome his opposition."

"Do you honestly believe that last part?" he asked cynically.

I had no answer ready for him, knowing that actually, I did not.

"Last night when the explosion occurred in the laboratory and I was afraid at first that Dad might have been injured or even killed," he went on after a little pause, "I felt as though I'd been a selfish heel even to consider taking part in the play when I knew what his feelings would be on the subject. That's why I couldn't discuss it with you afterwards; I'd have felt like a traitor to him if I had. But I realized this morning that that was only the emotionalism of the moment. I know now I've got to be in that play, regardless of everything. You see, Professor Barto told us a talent scout friend of his is coming down from New York to see it; and if he likes any of us, there may be just a chance . . ."

I understood the thought which he had left unspoken. "The theater is really in your blood, isn't it, Mark?" I asked.

He gave a brief, shaky laugh, the kind a man gives when he is recalling some unpleasant experience. "It's odd you should use that particular expression, Professor Laing," he remarked. "I said practically the same thing to Dad one day last fall when I wanted to enroll for Professor Barto's course in dramatic interpretation. I'm not actually in any of his classes, you know.

"He gave me a look I won't forget in a hurry—Dad,

I mean—then he said that if he thought that was the
case, he'd make me undergo one of those series of opera-
tions where they drain off every drop of blood in a
man's body and exchange it for new. I realized he didn't
mean that literally, of course; but I knew that what he
did mean was that he'd resort to any measures, no
matter how hard they were on either or both of us, to
destroy my interest in the stage. In fact—" his voice
dropped to an unsteady whisper "—I got the impression
that before he'd permit me to become an actor, he'd
rather see me dead."

I tried to convince him that he'd been letting his
imagination run away with him, and that his father
could have had no such thought in mind, but I wasn't
too sure that I succeeded. He left then, promising to
think over the advice I had given him; but I noticed
that he made no promise to follow it.

The thought of him and his problem remained with
me for a long time after he had gone. Although I
realized that I had no right to interfere between father
and son in a matter which was obviously none of my
affair and which in addition possessed all the character-
istics of potential dynamite, the fact that the boy had
turned to me for help had created in me a feeling of
responsibility for him which I found it impossible to
shake off. Yet I knew it would be worse than useless to
approach Eric Fordyce on the subject unless I was armed
with some understanding of what lay behind his violent
opposition to Mark's pursuing a theatrical career.

The thought flashed across my mind that perhaps, like
so many parents who were unsympathetic toward their
children's aspirations to the theater, he might feel that
his son was merely stage-struck, and possessed of no
genuine talent, and would therefore be wasting his time.
Whether this was true or not, I didn't know, but I
decided it would be advisable to find out before align-
ing myself too definitely on Mark's side. And the person
best in a position to give me such information ought to
be the man who was directing the play, Professor Antonio Barto.

Accordingly I cut my eleven o'clock lecture class—to
the gratification, I had no doubt, of some hundred and
fifty students in analytical psychology—and, having
once heard Barto say that he had a free period at that
time, went up to his office on the second floor of College
Hall on the chance of finding him there.

My knock at his door was answered by his invitation
to enter—given after an almost imperceptible hesi-
tancy—and I pushed the door open. But before I had
taken more than a step across the threshold I stopped,
having discovered not only that he already had a visitor,
but, from the breath of exotic perfume that seemed
fairly to permeate the room, that his visitor was of the
female gender.

"Sorry, Barto," I apologized, preparing to withdraw
again. "I didn't realize you weren't alone. I'll come
around some other time."

"How did you—" he began, then checked himself,

but his meaning was clear to me. He was wondering how I had known he had a visitor, forgetting, as do so many sighted people, that we who are blind have become accustomed to relying upon our other sensory perceptive faculties to tell us what the average man learns through his eyes. "Perhaps we can have lunch together, Professor Laing," he suggested, affably enough, but with, I felt, a poorly concealed anxiety to be rid of me. "I will call for you at your office at—shall we say one o'clock?"

I agreed to this arrangement and withdrew, wondering a little just who his visitor had been. I was almost certain she was not one of his students there to see him upon some school matter, not only because that cloying perfume hadn't been of the kind generally affected by our co-eds, but because, had she been, there would have been no reason for him to have become in any way discomfited by my unexpected intrusion. Neither, apparently, was she a personal friend to any appreciable degree, or he would have been having luncheon with her instead of being at liberty to make that arrangement with me. However, since the nature of Barto's feminine callers appeared to be no concern of mine, I dismissed the little episode from my mind and returned to my own office to wait for him.

Over luncheon at one of the campus "hash houses" an hour or so later, I put to him my question regarding Mark Fordyce, and was surprised by the warmth of his response.

"Young Marco!" he exclaimed, referring to the boy

affectionately by the Spanish form of his name. "You
ask me whether he possesses any genuine talent for acting? Genius would be a better and not inappropriate
word in his case. He has the true fire of the real artist!
Booth, Mansfield, Barrymore—he is of their class, or
will be when he has properly matured. Even now, with
the little training I have been privileged to give him in
odd moments . . ." His words trailed away in an enthus-
iasm which was plainly beyond his powers of expression.

"You have been giving him private coaching, then?"
I asked.

I sensed his Latin shrug, even though I was unable to
see it.

"Hardly anything so formal," he replied. "We have
spent a few evenings together in my rooms discussing
theater, and I have observed him at the university dramatic club, of which I am faculty advisor. But tell me,
my friend." His voice dropped to a more confidential
level. "Although Marco has never said so to me in words,
he has given me by his actions reason to believe that he
receives little sympathy at home in his desire to become
an actor. Is this the case?"

"I believe his father doesn't entirely approve of a
theatrical career for him," I replied cautiously, and
hoped Heaven would forgive me for this masterpiece of
understatement.

"Then this disapproval must be either overcome or
defied," Barto declared with a determination which implied that he would brook no interference. "Acting is

Marco's natural heritage. To deny it to him would be
as great a sin as to deny to the birds of the air their
right to sing. And I, Antonio Barto, shall see to it that
it is not denied, even if I have to—"

He broke off with the same self-conscious laugh he
had given when we had walked across campus together
the preceding evening and he had expressed himself so
forcefully on the American attitude toward art and
morality. "But I am permitting myself to be carried
away again by my emotions," he said apologetically.
"There are two people you must never take too literally, Professor Laing—a Latin and an actor, and I am
both. But I trust I have answered your question satis-
factorily?"

"You have," I told him with feeling.

As it developed, I was destined to have contact with
the affairs of young Mark Fordyce that day from still
another angle. When I returned home that afternoon
after the close of classes, I found Lee Laurence, one of
the girls in the Senior class, closeted with Deirdre.
Although she was a frequent visitor at the house, having
been a Freshman when Deirdre herself was a Senior at
the university, and was on a familiar footing with both
of us, she seemed a little disconcerted by my arrival,
and left soon thereafter.

"What's wrong with Lee?" I asked Deirdre after the
girl had gone. "Don't tell me she's afraid of failing in
psychology, and was here to ask you to plead her case
for her."

Deirdre laughed. "You flatter both yourself and your subject, Paddy," she told me. "I'm afraid that what Lee came to see me about is a great deal more important from her standpoint than whether she passes or fails in psychology." Then she sobered. "But I shouldn't laugh at her," she said contritely. "Affairs of the heart can be very painful to those concerned, even if they do sound a little amusing to other people."

"Have she and Mark been having a lovers' quarrel?" I inquired, knowing of the attachment that had existed between the girl and Mark Fordyce since the beginning of the school term the preceding fall.

"It's much worse than that," Deirdre replied. "Incredible as it may sound, it seems that recently Mark has become afflicted with what is known as the wandering eye. The—you should excuse the expression—lady involved," she suppressed another giggle, "is, according to Lee, 'a cheap, painted hussy who uses loud perfume and is old enough to be his mother.' She wanted to know what I thought she ought to do about the situation."

"What did you tell her?" I asked curiously.

"I told her that anything that was worth having was certainly worth fighting for."

"How unladylike!"

Deirdre leaned over the back of my chair and pretended to pull my hair. "I seem to recall that I practically had to do the proposing because you had some ridiculous notion about not having the right to ask me to marry you," she remarked, "and if you dare to imply that *I'm* not a lady, Patrick Laing . . ."

I surrendered unconditionally.

"A painted hussy who uses loud perfume," I repeated, chuckling a little over Lee's undoubtedly biased description of her rival. And then for no reason that I could account for logically, the memory of the exotic perfume worn by the woman who had been in Barto's office flashed across my mind. I had no grounds for supposing there might be any connection between the two, yet the idea that there was, persisted, while behind it skulked the uneasy suspicion that such a connection was not good. I began to feel a vague and disquieting distrust of Antonio Barto and his influence upon young Mark Fordyce.

CHAPTER III

The next few weeks drifted by uneventfully insofar as further developments in the affairs of the Fordyces were concerned. Lee dropped around at the house once or twice during that time, and I learned later from Deirdre that the girl's campaign to win Mark back had practically bogged down. He remained friendly enough, but he had apparently made it plain that he intended to keep that friendship upon a strictly platonic basis.

"What can you do, Paddy," Deirdre asked me after the second of Lee's visits, "when a man not only drops you for another woman, but then actually expects you to be interested and sympathetic when he tells you all about her?"

"I don't know, Derry," I answered, being in a somewhat flippant mood at the moment. "I've never been dropped for another woman. But tell Lee to cheer up. Men don't have too much sense when they're just past twenty."

"Neither," she retorted pointedly, "do they seem to have too much when they're past thirty."

I left that remark strictly alone.

As for Mark himself, I got the impression that he was avoiding me, for he made no further effort to discuss his theatrical problem with me, as I had been almost certain he would after our talk in my office that morning. I learned indirectly that he had accepted and was going on with the part in the play, but whether with or without his father's consent, I had no way of knowing.

I did, however, have one brief encounter with Eric Fordyce. It was a few days after the explosion in the laboratory when, as I was returning home from an evening class, I encountered him on his way back from the university chemistry laboratory, where he had evidently been putting in a few hours of extra work on his research experiment with his collaborator, Professor Fosdick. Since we were headed in the same direction, we continued the rest of the way together.

"I expect to be leaving here shortly, Laing," he remarked presently as we walked along. "My experimental work with Professor Fosdick is almost completed."

"I'm sorry to hear that," I replied with sincerity; for while the man's peculiar reserve had prevented him from becoming on very intimate terms with anybody, I had liked what little I had come to know of him. "I had hoped you might be interested in staying on as a regular member of the faculty."

"Ordinarily, I'd like nothing better," he admitted—a little wistfully, I thought. "But I feel that Mark needs a change. He's becoming restless here."

"I thought Mark was particularly happy at the university," I said in surprise.

"He'll be graduated from the university in June," he pointed out. "After that, he must decide what he wants to do with his life."

Since he had, figuratively, unlatched the door for me, I decided to risk pushing it open a little farther.

"Mark seems to be interested in the theater," I ventured, "and I've heard from other sources that he has genuine talent. Has he considered going on the stage as a career?"

The violence of Eric Fordyce's reaction startled me, even though I had been partially prepared for it.

"No!" he exclaimed. "That is the one thing he shall never do! Mark shall never go on the stage with my consent—or without it, if I am able to prevent it."

Then, as though realizing belatedly the force of his own words and fearing that they might have given offense, he apologized.

"Sorry, Laing," he said. "I hadn't meant to go off like that. It's merely that I can't see the theater as a fitting career for my son."

After that, he seemed lost in his own thoughts; but just before we reached his house, he spoke again.

"Laing," he said, and his voice sounded strangely tired, as though the weight of the years had suddenly descended upon him, "never undertake to interfere in other people's lives, just because an illogical quirk in the law has given you the power to do it. For the satisfaction it promises at the outset soon turns into a burden that is too great for any mortal man to bear."

The speech was a strange one, and he had uttered it almost as though it had been wrung from him by some secret torment which he was unable to bear any longer in silence. But he had not said enough to justify my asking him to say more, and so there was no way left open whereby I could try to help him.

I answered something—I had no idea what either then or later—and we said good night.

For a long time afterward I puzzled over what he had said to me and its possible application to Mark, for I had no doubt that in some way it concerned him. Then gradually it faded from my mind, and was all but forgotten.

For approximately three weeks then all was, if not actually serene, at least quiet. Had I not been so occupied with my own affairs—getting two classes of Senior students over the final hump before graduation, to say nothing of making out final grades for several other classes of both undergraduate and graduate students—I might have realized that this apparent calm was only the lull which precedes the storm. And then, as it was bound to, the storm broke.

I was preparing to leave my office for the day when, somewhat to my surprise, Mark stopped by to extend to Deirdre and me an invitation to attend the dress rehearsal of the Senior play, which was to be held that evening.

"I hope you'll both come," he went on with boyish

shyness. "Dress rehearsal is a little different from the actual performance—sort of extra special. The audience is made up only of people who have been personally invited by the cast and crew."

I thanked him and assured him that Deirdre and I would be very happy to attend. Then I asked, "Will your father be there, too, Mark?"

He hesitated. "I'm afraid not, Professor Laing," he admitted finally. "So far as I know, he isn't even aware that I'm in the play."

"You didn't tell him, then?"

"I couldn't," he answered. "He was worried over some difficulty he and Professor Fosdick were having with their experiment, and I didnt want to upset him further. After that straightened itself out, it was too late—I mean for Professor Barto to have got anybody to take my place in case Dad made me step out."

I couldn't help wondering whether most of that explanation hadn't been merely a convenient sop to his conscience, but I refrained from saying so.

The play was being presented in the drama department's little theater, a recently erected building on the edge of the campus. The auditorium was less than a quarter full when Deirdre and I arrived about fifteen minutes before the time the rehearsal had been scheduled to begin. Most of the audience were students, both male and female, but there was also a smattering of faculty members who spoke to us as we came in.

"What's the play to be, Paddy?" Deirdre inquired as

we found seats midway down the center aisle. "I haven't even heard."

"Marlowe's *Dr. Faustus*," I replied. "Mark is playing the title role."

"*Dr. Faustus*," she repeated pensively. "I hope the hell-fire will all be confined to the stage."

We had been seated only a few minutes when Lee Laurence came prancing up to us. "Hello, you two!" she greeted us gaily. "Mark said this morning he was inviting you, or I'd have asked you myself."

"I didn't know you had a part in the play, Lee," Deirdre said. "Should I tell you your costume looks very well, or would that be the wrong thing to say under the circumstances?"

"Just so you don't make any remarks about type casting," the girl answered with a light laugh, then explained for my benefit, "I'm one of the devils. How do you like my horns, Patrick?" She bent toward us.

I passed the tips of my fingers over the soft fluff of her bangs, where two tiny devil's horns nestled.

"Very becoming," I assured her. "You should try wearing them to class some day."

She giggled and, saying something about the rehearsal's being about ready to start, dashed off again.

"Lee seems unusually gay tonight," I observed to Deirdre. "Have she and Mark had a reconciliation?"

"Not that I know of," she replied doubtfully. "I'm afraid it's just an act she's putting on for his benefit. He's standing over by the door that leads backstage—

talking to a woman."

"*The* woman?"

"I imagine so." Deirdre paused a moment, then added, "And, Paddy, I'm afraid Lee's description of her was pretty close to the truth. She *is* a little—well, flamboyant in appearance, and she must be close to her middle thirties, although she's made up to look much younger."

Just then Barto came out upon the stage to make a brief curtain speech, and we were obliged to fall silent.

He spoke for barely a minute; then the play began. The speech of the Greek chorus which Christopher Marlowe had written for the opening had been omitted, so that the play started with Dr. Faustus alone in his study. Mark delivered his lines well, better than many professionals I had heard. The shy, immature schoolboy I had known seemed to have vanished, transformed into the elderly medieval scholar philosophizing upon the nature and purpose of his scholarship as he contemplated the forbidden necromantic lore. By the time the first scene had ended and he had made his exit amid a burst of enthusiastic applause from his audience, I found myself agreeing with Barto that the stage was the boy's natural heritage, and that to deny it to him would be a sin indeed.

"He's good!" Deirdre whispered to me under cover of the applause. "Even his gestures are the gestures of an old man! I wish his father were here to see him, Paddy. It might make him change his mind about allowing him to go on the stage professionally."

However, I doubted that. Remembering Eric Fordyce's impassioned outburst that evening when I had suggested the possibility of Mark's pursuing a theatrical career, I was convinced that talent or the lack of it had very little to do with the doctor's attitude in the matter.

The play progressed on a more or less even keel—most of the supporting players were woefully lacking in Mark's natural ability—up to the conjuring scene wherein Dr. Faustus, yielding to the temptation of the forbidden arts, has resolved to "try the uttermost magic can perform." Mark had repeated the long Latin incantation, and there came the burst of stage thunder heralding the first appearance of Mephistopheles. And then, before its echo had entirely died away, a voice spoke from the rear of the auditorium.

"Stop!" it commanded hoarsely. "Stop this play at once!"

There was a startled gasp from the audience and the rustle of people turning in their seats to discover who had caused the disturbance. Two or three co-eds giggled nervously, then fell abruptly silent.

Deirdre had turned with the others. "Merciful Heaven!" she gasped, clutching my arm. "Paddy, it's Dr. Fordyce! He looks angry enough to kill Mark!"

Eric Fordyce strode down the aisle, his footsteps echoing hollowly through the now otherwise silent theater. At sight of his father, Mark must have been stricken speechless, for he had made no effort to go on with his lines.

The dreadful silence continued until Dr. Fordyce must have been within a few rows of the front of the auditorium. Then a voice spoke from the stage.

"What is the meaning of this interruption?" it demanded. It belonged to Antonio Barto.

Eric Fordyce ignored him and addressed his son. "Take off that ridiculous get-up and put on your own clothes, Mark," he commanded with deadly calm. "You're coming with me."

"He shall not!" Barto denied, and now it was he who thundered. "Marco, remain where you are."

"Did you hear me, Mark?" Fordyce's voice had become as a blade of cold, tempered steel. "Do as I say."

There was another of those heart-breaking, leaden silences; then Mark Fordyce spoke.

"Very well, Dad," he said slowly and distinctly, so that everyone in the auditorium heard his words, "I'll do as you say—for the last time. But I warn you, I'll make you regret this if it's the last thing I ever do."

CHAPTER IV

Deirdre and I walked home from the little theater building in sober silence. When we were almost there, she spoke for the first time since we had left the auditorium.

"Dr. Fordyce shouldn't have done that," she said.

"No," I agreed, "it was the wrong move to make. Regardless of how much he disapproved of Mark's taking part in the play, he should never have humiliated the boy in public."

"I didn't mean that," Deirdre explained. "I was thinking of Professor Barto. When he saw that Mark was going to obey his father, his expression became terrible—almost murderous."

"That's the second man you've described tonight as having murder in his eye," I reminded her lightly.

"I know," she admitted. "But this time I mean it literally. It was as if some intense, burning hatred that he'd kept buried deep inside of him for a long time had suddenly broken through to the surface. Paddy, do you mind if we take a turn or two around the block before going into the house? I feel as if I need to walk to get the memory of him out of my mind."

For perhaps ten or fifteen minutes more, we continued to walk through the quiet night before turning in
at our own walk. As we were mounting the steps of the
porch, there came to us the sound of muffled sobbing. It
seemed to originate in the direction of the swing.

"What in the world—?" Deirdre began wonderingly.
"Why, it's Lee!" She released my arm and ran forward.
"What's the matter, honey?"

Lee choked on a final sob. "Derry, it's all my fault!"
she gulped. "I had to talk to somebody about it, so I
came here and waited for you and Pat to come home."

"What's all your fault?" Deirdre asked, uncompre-
hending. "Lee, what are you talking about?"

"What happened back there at the theater." The sobs
threatened to set in again. "I was the one who told Dr.
Fordyce about Mark's being in the play!"

Deirdre led her into the house. "Sit here in this big
chair and tell me all about it," she directed soothingly.
"Or do you want me to send Paddy away first?"

"No, let him stay," Lee managed between sniffles.
"Maybe he'll be able to think of some way I can patch
things up—if they *can* be patched up," she added
doubtfully.

She told us her story then. It began with her chanc-
ing to encounter Dr. Fordyce as she was on her way
back from classes to the women's dormitory that afternoon.

"He said that he hadn't seen me around with Mark

lately," she went on, "and he asked whether we'd had some sort of misunderstanding. I couldn't tell him it was all on account of That Woman, it would have sounded too childish; so I told him I supposed Mark had been too busy learning his part in the play to see much of anybody. I'd no idea he didn't already know about that."

"What did he say?" Deirdre asked.

"He didn't say anything at first," Lee replied. "I thought he looked at me rather strangely; only I supposed it was because he'd guessed I hadn't told him the exact truth about Mark and me. Then he asked me when the play was to be presented. I told him tomorrow night, and that the dress rehearsal was tonight. Even then I never suspected . . ."

"Of course you didn't!" Deirdre exclaimed comfortingly. "You're blaming yourself for something that was in no way your fault. Besides, maybe it all happened for the best. Dr. Fordyce was bound to find out sooner or later, and it would have been much worse if he had found out tomorrow night, and had made that scene during the actual performance. Now dry your eyes while I fix you a nice cup of tea." She hurried out of the room.

"Whether I was actually to blame or not," Lee said to me while we waited for Deirdre to return, "it was my cowardice in not telling Dr. Fordyce the truth this afternoon that caused all the trouble; and now I'm afraid Mark will think I did it on purpose, and he'll never forgive me for it. Do you suppose I ought to go over there, Pat, and try to explain?"

"No, Lee," I told her. "At least not tonight. There's nothing you or anyone could say that would help matters just now. Give Mark and his father time for a cooling off period; then offer your explanation. If Mark holds you responsible after that, he'll be less fair-minded than I think he is."

A minute or so later, Deirdre returned with the tea.

"Drink this and it'll make you feel better," she said to Lee. "Then after you've washed your face and powdered your nose, Paddy and I will walk you back to the dormitory."

It was ten minutes to eleven before the three of us finally left the house together; and since all women students living at the university dormitory were required to be in by eleven o'clock unless they had been granted a special late permission, we took the short cut across campus in order that Lee might get back in time. We were hurrying along the path that led between College Hall and the Fine Arts Building when the girl suddenly stopped dead in her tracks, and I heard her catch her breath with what sounded like painful sharpness.

"What's the matter, Lee?" I asked. "Are Derry and I walking too fast for you?"

"No," she answered, and her voice trembled a little, "it isn't that. It's up ahead there—Mark and That Woman! I can't pass them!"

"You can and you're going to," Deirdre said firmly. "This is no time to back down before either one of them. Do you want to act like a coward and make Mark think you really did know what you were doing when you told his father about his being in the play? Anyway," she added as Lee continued to hesitate, "it's dark where they're standing. We can pretend we didn't recognize them and pass without speaking unless Mark speaks to us first."

This suggested compromise worked, and we proceeded along the path in a somewhat grim silence.

We passed the place where Mark and his companion were standing without a word being spoken on either side. There was no way, of course, of being sure whether they had recognized us or not. But I suspected that they had, for as we came abreast of them, I received the impression that they drew farther back against the building beside which they were standing, while their eyes watched us anxiously; fearful, perhaps, that Deirdre or Lee would give some sign of recognition.

I was also conscious of one other thing. The woman was wearing a heavy perfume, a heady, unusual scent there could be no mistaking. It was the same perfume that had been worn by the woman who had been in Barto's office when I had gone there that morning three weeks before.

After we had left Lee at the dormitory, I mentioned this matter of the perfume to Deirdre. "Of course," I finished, "I realize there may be absolutely no connection between the two. Probably hundreds of women use that same perfume."

Somewhat to my surprise, Deirdre disagreed with me. "Not *that* perfume," she replied. "It's too heavy for the discriminating woman unless she happens to be a very unusual type, and too expensive for the other kind."

"Was the woman you saw talking to Mark this evening a very unusual type?" I asked.

She considered a moment before she answered; then "Not in the way I meant," she said finally. "If you want my opinion, Paddy, she didn't buy that perfume for herself, but some man bought it for her."

"Mark?"

"Hardly. He's too young and inexperienced to have selected that particular scent. More likely it was an older man—Professor Barto, for instance."

There are times when Deirdre's understanding of masculine nature positively amazes me.

"You're assuming, then, that she *was* the woman who was in Barto's office?" I inquired.

"Yes, I suppose I am," she admitted. "It would be too much of a coincidence otherwise. Paddy, what do you suppose it all means?"

"Probably only that she's someone Mark met through Barto, and became infatuated with," I replied. "So even if the two women are one and the same, there's nothing in the least unusual or mysterious about the circumstance."

But again Deirdre disagreed with me, and this time

I was given an example of her understanding of feminine nature.

"I'm afraid there is," she said soberly. "If this woman were a close enough friend of Professor Barto's for him to buy her expensive presents like that—and that perfume did smell terribly expensive—she wouldn't run the risk of endangering that friendship by encouraging Mark. And if she isn't a close friend of Barto's . . ."

"And if she isn't . . .?" I prompted when she didn't go on.

"I'm not sure," she replied. "Maybe I'm entirely wrong, but I've a suspicion Professor Barto gave her that perfume, and probably other expensive presents as well, as a bribe to get her deliberately to encourage Mark. Oh, I've no reason for thinking so, I know; and even if I did have, it still wouldn't make sense. What reason would he have for doing a thing like that in the first place? What could he hope to gain by it?"

"For that matter," I observed, smiling a little at the lengths to which her active imagination had already carried her, "what reason have we to assume that Barto did give her the perfume? Remember, that part was only a supposition to begin with."

"Yes, I know," she admitted. "But somehow I can't get over the feeling that there's more behind all this than appears on the surface; that it's all part of some crazy plot that would make a lot of sense if we only knew how to look at it. Ever since we left the theater building tonight, I've had a queer Irish hunch that what happened back there, instead of being the climax of the situation, was really only the beginning; that ever since it happened—perhaps even long before—certain forces have been gathering that will very shortly come to a head."

They did come to a head even sooner than she had expected, and in a way more horrible than either of us could have foreseen. That night Dr. Fordyce's laboratory, as well as all that was in it, was completely destroyed by fire.

CHAPTER V

The fire broke out around one o'clock in the morning, and burned with a fury so intense that the place had become a raging inferno almost before it was discovered. Even as far away as our living room, where Deirdre and I had gone upon being awakened by the raucuous clanging of the fire-fighting apparatus and the shouts of the men as they strove to subdue it, we could hear the fierce crackling of the flames and feel the heat of them, like the panting breath of some wild beast.

Whatever hope the firemen might have had of saving the laboratory itself or anything it contained must have been given up practically from the beginning. The best they could do was ply the outside of the building and its immediate surroundings with water in order to keep the fire from spreading.

It was while Deirdre and I sat uneasily in the living room, not sure whether or not we would be obliged to evacuate our own home, that one of the firemen came across the intervening lawn to our side porch and knocked upon the French doors.

"Do you happen to know whether the people are

away over there, buddy?" he asked when I had answered. "We've pounded on both the front and back doors, but we can't get any answer."

"They haven't gone away so far as I know," I replied. "Dr. Eric Fordyce and his son live there." Then, as an unpleasant possibility crossed my mind, I asked, "Is it possible that they could have been overcome by smoke, and aren't able to answer?"

"It hardly seems likely," the fireman answered doubtfully. "The house is too far away from the garage where the fire is for that much smoke to have drifted in. Still, you never can tell. Maybe I'd better force an entrance and make sure."

He started to turn away; then he hesitated. "Would you mind going in there with me, buddy?" he asked. "It's always best to have somebody along that knows the family on a job like this."

I called to Deirdre to let her know where I was going; then I accompanied the fireman.

"Did the doc keep much gasoline stored in there, that you know of?" he inquired as I followed him back across the lawn.

I explained that the garage had been converted into a laboratory for chemical experiments.

"Then that explains it!" he exclaimed. "Nothing but gasoline or chemicals could burn like that. Lucky for him he wasn't working in there when this thing started. He might've been burnt to a cinder before he could have got out."

A crowd, drawn by the weird fascination of the un-leashed demon of destruction, had gathered in front of the house, but it was prevented from going any nearer to the source of the fire by a cordon of police. Even at that distance—the garage-laboratory was a good hun-dred feet to the rear—the air was scorched with the hot breath of the flames and acrid with the smell of smoke.

The fireman forced a way for us through the tightly packed crowd, which parted unwillingly to let us through, and we mounted the porch steps together.

"Seems I'll not have to force an entrance after all," he remarked a second or two later. "The front door's unlocked."

He pushed it open and stepped into the short hallway beyond. I followed.

"The bedrooms'll be on the second floor, I suppose," he muttered. "Where are the stairs?"

"They go up from the living room, on the left," I told him. Although I had never been in Dr. Fordyce's house before, I knew that all the houses in the block had been built from the same architectural plan.

He crossed the living room and started up the stairs with me close behind him, guiding myself by the sound of his footsteps.

"Anybody up here?" he shouted as we reached the second floor hall.

There was no answer.

He turned toward the front of the house, and I heard him open a door, then click on a light switch.

"Nobody in this room," he reported. "The bed hasn't even been slept in. Let's try the next one."

I stepped aside to permit him to enter it ahead of me.

"Whose room is this?" he demanded a moment later.

"Mark's—the son's—I believe," I answered. "Why?"

"Looks as though he left it in something of a hurry, the way he's left those bureau drawers pulled open," he replied. "He must have been packing a suitcase to take with him, too, from the looks of them. Anyway, he's not here now. Well, that leaves only the back room."

But the back room, which turned out to be a small study instead of a third bedroom, was also empty.

"Looks as if you were wrong, buddy, about this Dr. Fordyce and his son not having gone away," the fireman remarked as we descended the stairs. "Got any ideas where they might be reached?"

"No definite ideas," I told him. "But if you like, I'll go home and call several possible places where they might have gone."

"I wish you would," he said. "Somebody ought to let a man know when his property's on fire."

Back in my own home, I told Deirdre what we had found, particularly of the discovery in Mark's room.

"Oh, Paddy!" she exclaimed in distress. "Do you realize what's happened? Mark and his father must have had a dreadful quarrel after they got back from the theater, and now Mark's run away! Have you any idea where he might have gone?"

"My first guess would be to his friend, Barto," I replied. "I'll call the men's dormitory where Barto lives, and find out whether he's there."

But although the dormitory operator rang his phone a dozen times, there was no answer.

"I was just thinking," Deirdre said, troubled. "That woman he was with when we passed him on campus: You don't suppose . . ?"

"Hardly," I answered. "I doubt if Mark's the sort to indulge in that kind of escapade, even in his present mood. He's probably spending the night with one of his friends on campus. But since I can't very well canvass all of the men's dormitories for him at this time of night, I'll let him go and try to locate his father."

Knowing that when a man is in grief or trouble, his best anodyne is work, I dialed the university's exchange number and asked the switchboard operator to ring the chemistry building for me. But after a minute, she reported that there was no answer.

"Maybe he's at Professor Fosdick's house, seeing that they're working together," Deirdre suggested hopefully.

I thought the possibility none too likely, but I gave it a try. This time I at least got an answer to my ring.

"Fordyce?" Professor Fosdick, the head of our chemistry department, repeated sleepily and a little crossly when I had asked my question. "No, he's not here, Laing. Isn't he at home? Why the devil must you talk to him in the middle of the night?"

"His laboratory's on fire," I explained. "A member of the fire department asked me to locate him if I could."

That brought him wide awake in a hurry. "Oh, good Lord!" he exclaimed. "Fordyce had some valuable stuff in there. Were they able to save any of it?"

"I'm afraid not," I answered. "They had all they could do to keep the fire from spreading." I rang off before he could think of any more questions.

"Fosdick doesn't know where he is," I reported to Deirdre. "And, I'm afraid, neither do I. I was never on sufficiently intimate terms with the man to know what friends he's made since he came here, if he made any. Probably the best way to locate him will be to have a call for him put out over the local radio station. I'll mention it to that fireman when he comes back."

But the fireman didn't come back for several hours. The cool freshness of dawn was in the air when at last there came a second knock at the French doors. I went to answer it.

"It's me again, buddy," the fireman announced. He sounded infinitely tired, as I had no doubt that he was. "Have any luck locating the son?"

"No," I admitted; then, realizing how his question had been phrased, "Does that mean you've got in touch with Dr. Fordyce?"

He didn't answer directly. "Could you identify this Dr. Fordyce if you saw him?" he asked instead.

"I'm afraid not," I replied, and explained about my blindness.

I could feel him staring at me in blank incredulity. "And all the time you were over there with me, I never so much as suspected you couldn't see!" he exclaimed. "Well, I'll be damned!"

He returned to the matter that had brought him. "Is there anybody else here who could identify Fordyce?" he inquired.

"My wife could," I replied, even then not guessing what awful purpose lay behind his question. "I'll call her."

"No, don't," he stopped me. "This is hardly a job for a lady. What's happened is, we've found a body in there where the fire was, and we think it might be his."

CHAPTER VI

Later that morning, Deirdre and I got the details of the tragedy over the radio. After the fire had burned itself out and the ruins had cooled sufficiently, the fire chief and two of his men had gone inside to take inventory of the damage done and to make sure there was no danger of a second outbreak. There, to their horror, they had discovered the charred body of a man lying in the middle of the floor, its position suggesting that he had been overcome by smoke or fumes from the burning chemicals before he had been able to make his escape from the building. The body had later been identified by Professor Mortimer Fosdick as that of Dr. Eric Fordyce.

"It's all so horrible!" Deirdre moaned, snapping off the radio. "Not only Dr. Fordyce's having to die like that, but—poor Mark! Now he'll have to remember all his life that the last time he was with his father, they quarreled."

I had to agree with her that in all probability, this would be the case.

It was a relief to me when Lee Laurence came over

just before it was time for me to leave for my classes at the university, for I hadn't relished the idea of leaving Deirdre alone with the thought of that tragedy next door to keep her company.

"I'm cutting classes for the day," Lee announced. "When Mark comes back, he's going to need someone he can turn to, and I'd sort of like to be around."

Once more I marveled at the understanding of women.

"How did you know Mark was missing?" I asked her.

"They said so over the radio," she replied. "They've asked anybody who's seen him or who knows where he is to get in touch with the police immediately."

"The police!" Deirdre echoed, startled.

"The police will be nominally in charge until after the inquest," I explained. "There has to be an inquest into every case of violent death."

When I arrived at College Hall, I found that news of the tragedy had spread throughout the university, and the classes fairly buzzed with it. After the first two periods, I gave up attempting to lecture and resorted to impromptu written quizzes, much to the disgust of the young instructor who acts as my assistant, since he knew it would fall to his lot to have to grade them afterwards.

As I was about to go out for lunch at the end of the morning session, I encountered Professor Fosdick in the hall. He was a fussy little man, not accustomed to the sort of ordeal he had been obliged to undergo earlier that morning, and it had upset him considerably. He was apparently attempting to regain his emotional equilibrium by giving everyone he met a detailed description of his experience.

"I tell you, Laing, it was revolting!" he exclaimed when he had buttonholed me. "The man was burned to a cinder—literally to a cinder! And the smell! Ugh!"

I reminded him as tactfully as I could that we were both about to go out for lunch.

"Sorry," he apologized. "I forgot. I'm not having any lunch myself. Couldn't, you know, after—" He broke off and changed the subject with what with him passed for subtle diplomacy. "Incidentally, Dr. Fordyce's death isn't the only occurrence that's upset the even tenor of our ways here at the university this morning. I suppose you've heard?"

"You mean what happened during the play rehearsal last night?" I inquired.

"That wasn't what I had in mind," he replied, "although it did, in a sense, involve the same person. Barto of the dramatics department didn't put in an appearance to take charge of his classes this morning, and he sent no excuse. When the dean's office tried to contact him by telephone, there was no answer from his apartment. Do you imagine his—er—apparent disappearance could be in any way connected with that incident at the rehearsal?"

"Possibly," I conceded guardedly. "He's a more or less temperamental sort; he may not have felt in the mood to conduct classes this morning, and simply have neglected to notify the office."

"I understand it was Dr. Fordyce who caused that commotion last night," Fosdick rambled on, unable to keep away for long from the subject that was uppermost in his mind. "Something about his objection to Mark's having taken part in the play without his consent, wasn't it? Do you suppose there could have been any connection between it and what happened to him later?"

"If you're suggesting that his anger over discovering that his son had done something contrary to his known wishes was hot enough to have caused spontaneous combustion and so started the fire in his laboratory," I retorted, determined that he wasn't going to get any information on the subject out of me, "I'm afraid the possibility is somewhat remote."

I then left him sputtering over what he obviously considered my indecent flippancy.

I decided to go home for lunch that day instead of eating at one of the campus restaurants, as I usually did. There were two reasons for this decision: First, I wished to avoid probable catechisms about the fire on the part of my colleagues, and second, I wanted to learn whether Mark had returned yet.

He had not, but I found another visitor waiting for me in my living room. He was Detective Lieutenant Kenneth McDermott, a friend and associate of long standing, since I had been able to render him some slight assistance in the past on two or three murder cases he had been called upon to investigate.

"I won't hold you up any longer than necessary, Pat, for I know you've got to get back to your classes in an hour," he said when we had shaken hands. "But I've a couple of questions about this Fordyce affair that somebody's got to answer, and since you were his nearest neighbor—the house on the other side appears to be vacant—it looks as though you're elected."

I assured him that I would be glad to answer his questions to the best of my ability. At the same time, however, I couldn't help wondering why a full lieutenant should have been assigned to a case which, on the face of it, appeared to be merely a routine matter.

"How well did you know Dr. Fordyce?" he asked first.

"Not very well," I admitted. "He wasn't particularly sociable. Not in any churlish sense of the word; he was simply reserved. I knew his son, Mark, much better. He's in one of my classes at the university."

"What's he like?"

"A nice, likable lad, and a good student. His father's death's going to be an ugly shock to him when he learns of it."

McDermott offered no comment on this. His next question, however, surprised me a little, although I tried to tell myself that it had been prompted simply by my own remark.

"How did he and his father hit it off together?" he asked. "Were their relations generally congenial?"

"In many ways, they seemed much closer than the average father and son," I replied, selecting my words with care. "That's why Dr. Fordyce's death is going to be such a heavy blow to the boy."

"Did they generally see eye to eye on everything?"

Again I found myself becoming on my guard. "Do any two people ever see eye to eye on everything?" I countered. "Naturally they had some differences of opinion. What father and son haven't?"

McDermott clucked his tongue in disapproval. "Pat, you should know better than to hedge with the police," he chided. "But in case it's bothering you, I already know about that little episode last night when Fordyce crashed into the play rehearsal and literally dragged his son home by the scruff of the neck. What I want to find out from you is, just how deeply was the boy likely to have resented that?"

I didn't like either the question or the way he had put it. Neither did I like the feeling it gave me that there was more behind it than met the ear.

"Before we go any further, you'd better tell me just what you're driving at, Mac," I suggested. "If you're entertaining any far-fetched notion that Mark may have set fire to the laboratory as an act of retaliation for the theater episode, not knowing his father was in there, you can dismiss it."

"We've no actual proof yet that the fire was set," he replied, "although we know from a process of simple logic that it must have been." He paused, while I waited wordlessly for him to go on.

"This morning when the coroner performed the autopsy," he resumed at last, "he didn't find any smoke in the lungs, such as should have been there if death had been caused by suffocation or even if the doctor had been overcome by smoke and then burned to death. That led him to make a more thorough examination of the body than he'd have done ordinarily."

Again he paused. This time I was unable to remain silent until he was ready to continue.

"What did he find?' I demanded, and was surprised by the tenseness of my own voice.

"We found," McDermott replied, "that the cartilage of the windpipe and esophagus was badly bruised, as though they'd been squeezed by a pair of powerful hands. Fordyce had died of suffocation, all right; but it wasn't from the smoke. It was by strangulation."

CHAPTER VII

For a moment I felt as though a constriction of some kind had fastened itself about my own throat.

"But what has this to do with Mark?" I forced myself to ask the question, although I was already certain what McDermott's answer would be.

However, instead of replying directly, he put another question of his own which at first seemed wholly irrelevant.

"Pat, what is young Fordyce's middle name?" he inquired.

"Anthony," I replied, wondering why that should interest him.

"M. A. F.," he muttered to himself, as though I had just corroborated some doubtful point for him. Then he explained.

"While some of the boys from headquarters and I were going over the remains of the laboratory for possible clues," he began, "we came across a man's soft felt hat. By one of those freak accidents that sometimes happen, a set of metal shelves had broken loose from the wall and fallen across it before the fire got to it, so that it was hardly even scorched. The initials, M. A. F., were stamped inside on the sweat-band."

"There's nothing unusual about a hat of Mark's being found in his father's laboratory," I pointed out. "He might have left it there at any time."

"On the floor?" he asked significantly.

I remained silent.

"I'm afraid it's no use, Pat," McDermott said not unkindly. "There's a pretty sizable pile of evidence stacking up against the boy, and you can't brush it aside. In addition to the hat, there's that affair that happened at the theater last night. I've talked to several people who were there, and they've all quoted young Fordyce as having told his father he'd make him regret what had taken place if it was the last thing he ever did. In view of what happened afterwards, that sounds mighty like a murder threat. Then the boy's running away hasn't helped his case any, either."

I had been thinking furiously while he talked. Now I believed I had discovered a point to counter his argument.

"Wait a minute, Mac," I commanded. "You said Dr. Fordyce's throat had the appearance of having been squeezed by a pair of powerful hands. That lets Mark out immediately. His hands are rather small and slender, almost like a girl's, and I imagine not particularly strong. Besides, he's smaller in every way than his father was. It's inconceivable that he could have overpowered a man who was about four inches taller and at least thirty pounds heavier than he is."

"He was also about thirty years older," McDermott observed dryly. "And that, believe me, can be a handicap, even against a much lighter and smaller opponent."

But I wasn't ready to give up yet.

"You asked me a few minutes ago," I began afresh, "just how deeply Mark was likely to have resented his father's dragging him away from the play rehearsal last night. I didn't answer your question then, but I'll do it now: He did resent it very deeply, I'll not attempt to deny that, but not deeply enough for it to have driven him to commit murder. Mark loved his father; he'd never have raised his hand against him, no matter what the provocation. Why, when a small explosion occurred at the laboratory about three weeks ago, the boy was almost beside himself for fear that his father might have been injured in it."

"You say there was an explosion at the laboratory three weeks ago?" McDermott asked quickly, and something in his tone made me suspect what was passing through his mind.

"Yes," I answered. "But you can't link that up with last night's tragedy. It was an accident, pure and simple. Dr. Fordyce himself explained that it had been caused by the explosion of a test-tube he'd been heating."

"I've no doubt it was an accident that time," he replied in that same dry tone of voice he had used before. "But it gave young Mark an opportunity to see just how easily such an accident could occur, and to realize what a perfect cover-up it would make for a murder."

I perceived then that instead of helping the boy, I had only added to the weight of the evidence against him.

"You're determined to prove him guilty, aren't you, Mac?" I asked. "Is there nothing I can say or do that will induce you to give him at least the benefit of the doubt?"

He remained silent for the space of perhaps half a minute; then:

"Yes, there is, Pat," he said soberly. "You can help me find him, and after he's been found, convince him that his best course is to tell the whole truth about what happened last night. If he's innocent, as you believe, he should be able to prove it."

I agreed with that only in part, for I had known too many innocent men in the past who had been unable to prove their own innocence unassisted. However, I did promise to do my utmost to help find Mark Fordyce, and when he was found, to prevail upon him if I could to hold back nothing from the police. After that, Mc-Dermott left.

I went out onto the side porch, where I knew Deirdre and Lee were waiting for me.

"What was that all about, Paddy?" Deirdre asked. "Does the lieutenant want you to help them find Mark?"

"Yes," I answered. "But that wasn't the primary purpose of his visit." I repeated to them then what

McDermott had told me.

When I explained how Dr. Fordyce's death had been murder instead of accident, they were both speechless with horror and incredulity; but when I came to the part involving Mark, Lee became voluble with indignation.

"It's not so!" she cried, and her voice trembled with the enormity of the outrage. "They're crazy to believe a thing like that! Mark would never have harmed his father, no matter how angry he might have been with him!"

"That's what I tried to impress upon the lieutenant, Lee," I replied, "but he says there's too much evidence against Mark to be ignored. He pointed out that if Mark is really innocent, his best course is to come forward and help clear himself of suspicion."

"And you promised to help find him?' she demanded. "Pat, you mustn't! If you do, they'll only—what's the word?—railroad him for his father's murder!"

"Wait, Lee," Deirdre intervened. "The lieutenant is right, and so is Paddy: Mark has got to be found for his own good. If he isn't, it'll only make him appear more guilty."

"I don't care," the girl retorted stubbornly. "I'd rather have him *appear* guilty than be *found* guilty. Do you think I want him to be sent to jail—maybe worse—for a crime he didn't commit?"

I tried another line of argument.

"Do you want him to be hiding from the police all

the rest of his life?" I asked her. "To live like a hunted animal, running from one dark corner to another because he's afraid that if he stays in any one place for more than a little while, someone may recognize him! Afraid to make friends for fear one of them will betray him, afraid that every hand laid upon his shoulder may be the hand of the law come to place him under arrest? And at last run down, as would be bound to happen eventually, when it's too late for him to prove his innocence?"

The picture I painted frightened her, as I had intended that it should.

"But if he *is* found—or gives himself up—what will happen then?" she asked fearfully.

"I don't know," I admitted. "It will all depend on what he may tell us. But at least he'll have a fighting chance to save himself. He has none now."

She remained silent for a long minute; then she said in a tight little voice, "Pat, you must promise me one thing; that if you do find him, you'll get him to tell you his story before you say anything to the police. Then if you find it won't help, or maybe even make things look worse for him, you've got to let him go again.'

I started to protest that I had no right to make such a promise, but she interrupted me.

"If you don't," she declared desperately, "I won't tell you how you can get in touch with him."

"You know where he is?" I demanded in amazement,

for it was the last thing I had expected.

"Not exactly," she acknowledged, "but I know how to find out. Oh, Pat, if you really believe in his innocence, you'll make that promise!"

I made it.

Lee's attitude changed as if by magic. Her hostility melted away, and she became almost conspiratorial.

"Last night after you took me back to the dormitory," she began, "I sat at my window without turning on the light, just looking out and—well, thinking. After a little while I saw Mark and That Woman come down the path to the main entrance to the campus. She went on up the street and out of sight, but he stayed where he was, as if he were waiting for her to come back.

"After about five minutes, she did come back, but this time she wasn't walking; she was driving a light-colored sedan. She drew up to the curb, and Mark got in beside her. I noticed then for the first time that he had a suitcase with him.

"Maybe she drove him to the railroad station, or maybe he's with her now." Her voice faltered over that latter thought; then she hurried on, as if to put it behind her. "Anyway, she can tell you where to find him, and you've got to make her do it."

Mentally I called myself an idiot for not having thought of that possibility in the first place. But in the rush of events following the fire, I had completely forgotten about the woman in whose company Mark had been the evening before when we had passed him on campus.

"Do you know her name and where she lives?" I asked Lee.

"Her name is Nora Hilton, and she lives at a boarding house over on Spruce Street," she replied, and gave me its number. "Mark told me that. He also told me she's an actress from New York, who's here resting between shows. 'Resting,' she calls it!"

I smiled, understanding that the term was a polite one used by theatrical people meaning out of a job. What puzzled me, however, was that Nora Hilton should have come to our town to do her "resting," when she could have done it just as well in New York, and with a much better chance of finding new employment.

Since I had only one lecture and one clinic class that afternoon, I phoned my assistant to take charge of them for me. Then I had Deirdre drive me to the address Lee had given me, leaving Lee herself at the house on the off chance that Mark might return home while we were gone.

The neighborhood where the boarding house was located was one that had once been considered fashionable, but which had fallen into leaner ways as the city had grown and its original occupants had moved farther uptown or into the suburbs. I left Deirdre to wait in the car, crossed the narrow pavement, and mounted the three stone steps with their rusted, wrought-iron balustrades.

My first ring went unanswered, but my second brought to the door a woman with a sharp tongue and a suspicious manner.

"If you're lookin' for a room, I ain't got none vacant," she snapped before I could so much as open my mouth.

"I'm not in search of a room, only of a roomer," I hastened to assure her. "Miss Nora Hilton. Is she in?"

"No, she's not," the woman replied ungraciously, and I heard the hinges of the door give a preliminary creak.

"Do you happen to know where I can find her, or when she'll be back?" I pressed.

"I don't know either one." The reply came grudgingly. "She went out of here last night, takin' a week-end bag with her. Her room rent was paid up, so I didn't bother to ask her where she was goin' or whether she'd be back or not."

I hadn't realized how much I'd been counting on what Nora Hilton might be able to tell me until I found myself confronted with the possibility of not talking to her at all.

"Isn't there anyone here whom she might have told where she was going?" I made a final, desperate try.

Instead of answering directly, the landlady put a question of her own. "Say," she demanded suspiciously, "are you a friend of hers, or has she been up to something she shouldn't ought to?"

"I've never had the pleasure of meeting Miss Hilton personally," I explained. "I've come on behalf of a mutual friend."

I could feel her staring at me with growing curiosity. "Say, you talk just like one o' them college professors out at the university," she observed; then, as though this had been in my favor, her manner softened a trifle. "Nora's got a roommate, Hazel Phipps, and she's in just now," she volunteered. "You can come in and talk to her if you want to. Maybe she can tell you what you want to know about Nora."

I thanked her, and she led me into a narrow hall that smelled of stale cooking odors and laundry.

"Wait there in the living room while I tell her you're here," she directed, and I heard her throw open a door on the left. "I don't allow men callers to go upstairs to my women boarders' rooms."

I went into the living room and waited.

After a few minutes there came the staccato click of high heels descending the uncarpeted stairs, and a younger woman entered the room, preceded by a blast of perfume; not the scent worn by Nora Hilton, but one equally strong if not, as Deirdre would have expressed it, as expensive-smelling.

"Hello, chum," she greeted me in a voice which I suspected had been made deliberately sultry and inviting by careful practice. "The Queen says you want to talk to me about Nora."

"Yes, Miss Phipps," I corroborated, rising. "I'm trying to locate her in the interest of a young friend of both of us. Can you tell me where she's gone?"

"There came a sound which I judged was caused by her dropping into a broken-springed, upholstered chair similar to the one I had located while I waited for her to come down, but which was more suggestive of one sack of potatoes being tossed upon another.

"Who's the friend?" she demanded.

"Mark Fordyce."

"The kid they're tryin' to locate over the radio on account of his old man gettin' killed last night?"

"The same," I affirmed. "I've reason to believe Miss Hilton may be able to tell me where I can find him."

"I'll say she can!" she muttered in an aside which I evidently wasn't intended to hear; then in suspicion not unlike the landlady's, "Look here, chum; you wouldn't happen to be a detective, would you?"

"No," I answered. "My name is Patrick Laing, and I'm a close friend of Mark's." I had a sudden inspiration. "I've got to find him before the police do."

That apparently convinced her that I was to be trusted.

"All right," she decided, "I'll tell you what you want to know—or as close to it as I can come. He's with Nora now, or at least he ought to be. She left here some time last evening to meet him."

She paused, then made her crowning announcement:

"They were running away together to be married."

CHAPTER VIII

"*Married!*" I echoed the word stupidly.

"That's what I said," she affirmed. "What's the matter? Didnt you ever hear the word before? People have been doin' it for years."

"Forgive me, Miss Phipps," I said as soon as I had recovered from the first stunning shock of what she had told me, "but I was under the impression that Miss Hilton was—er—considerably older than Mark. Why should she want to marry such a mere boy?"

She laughed tolerantly. "I'll say she's older than Mark!" she exclaimed with feeling. "Why, Nora Hilton's been twenty-nine ever since I knew her, and the Lord only knows how long before that. Maybe that was the reason she was willing to marry him; maybe she was getting desperate, and the kid looked like her last chance. I don't know."

"Did she tell you where they were going after they were married?" I asked.

"No," she admitted. "I wasn't around when she left, but she wrote me a note and pinned it to my pillow. I found it when I got in a little after twelve. Here, you can read it if you want to." There was a faint rustle of paper as she produced it.

"I'm afraid I'll have to ask you to read it to me, Miss Phipps," I said apologetically. "You see, I'm blind."

I could fairly hear her jaw drop open. "My Gawd!" she gasped before she could stop herself. "And here I've been puttin' on my best cheese cake all for nothin'!"

Then she recovered herself. "You sure had me fooled, chum," she confided with a light laugh at her own expense. "Here I was, thinkin' you were keepin' your eyes on a level with my face simply because you were that kind of a guy. Well, anyway, here's what the note says." She unfolded it and read aloud:

" 'Dear Hazel: By the time you read this, I'll prob-ably be Mrs. Mark Fordyce—Heaven help me! My little boy friend finally got to the point of asking me to marry him tonight, and I want to go through with it before one or the other of us loses our nerve. Wish me luck. I'll be back in a day or two. Nora.

" 'P. S. If Tony Barto calls, tell him to keep his shirt on, and that he'll hear from me tomorrow.'

"Nothing there to tell you where they've gone, I'm afraid," she concluded. "But she says she'll be back in a day or two; and anyway, she's got to come back to get the rest of her clothes—she only took a week-end bag with her. But in the meantime, maybe Tony Barto can tell you where they are, since she said she was going to get in touch with him."

"Who is this Tony Barto?" I asked, concealing the

fact that I already knew in the hope that she might tell me something which would explain the relationship between him and Nora Hilton.

"He used to be an actor and small-time director she knew back in New York—which was where I first met her three years ago when I had bright ideas about going on the stage," she threw in parenthetically. "But now he's given up that end of the business, and has got a job teaching kids like Mark to act out at the university. I don't know his address, but they ought to be able to give it to you out there."

"Is he a close friend of Miss Hilton's?" I inquired, trying not to sound too interested.

"Well, now, that depends a lot on how you look at it,' she replied judiciously. "She used to play up to him in a big way back in the old days so that he'd give her parts in the plays he was doing; but there was never anything between them, if thats what you mean. Tony's a queer sort; never seemed to bother much about women, although I suspect he's known some fancy ones in his time. It's a funny thing, though . . ." She paused, as though lost in some private contemplation.

"You were saying . . ?" I prompted when she didn't go on.

"Oh, yes." She brought herself up with a jerk. "I was about to say that when she first came here three months ago and looked me up to ask if she could room with me, she told me Tony Barto had sent for her, that he'd said he had a job for her. Yet so far as I know, she hasn't worked a single day since she's been here, although right away she blossomed out in the kind of fancy clothes and expensive perfume you don't buy in Wanamaker's basement."

"Maybe she'd saved some money while she was living in New York," I suggested.

She laughed at that. "It's easy to tell you've never been on the stage, chum," she commented.

I asked Miss Phipps one final question: Did she happen to know whether it was through Barto that Nora Hilton had met Mark Fordyce? When she replied that she believed this was so, I thanked her for her assistance, and left.

As we drove away from the house, I repeated the interview in detail to Deirdre.

"Poor Lee," she murmured when I had finished. "I'm afraid she's going to take the news of Mark's marriage rather badly. Have we got to tell her right away?"

"I'll leave that strictly up to you," I told her. "If you think it would be better to wait until after Mark's been found, we can wait. Her knowing or not knowing doesn't affect the case in any way."

"But I believe there may be something else that does!" Deirdre exclaimed suddenly. "Paddy, did Miss Phipps tell you what time it was when she found Nora Hilton's note?"

I thought back. "Yes," I answered after a moment. "She said she found it pinned to her pillow when she came in a little after twelve o'clock last night."

"Which means that Nora Hilton must have gone away with Mark some time earlier than that," Derry summarized. "Probably at the time when Lee saw her pick him up in the automobile a little after eleven o'clock. But the fire in Dr. Fordyce's laboratory didn't break out until after one. Don't you see what it means, Paddy? Mark's got an alibi!"

"You're right!" I exclaimed, perceiving what she meant. "They left too early for him to have committed the murder and set fire to the laboratory before they started, and too late for him to have done it after they came back. With the three-day license application law in this state, they'd have had to drive across the state line to be married, which means they couldn't have got back before two o'clock, at the earliest. At least," I added, "we'll hope it works out that way."

"Why, what do you mean?" Derry asked. "It's got to work out that way—doesn't it?"

"Not if they didn't actually go through with their marriage plans," I replied. "And we won't know whether they did or not until we've located them—or at least one of them. Derry, drive me back to the graduate men's dormitory on campus, where Barto has his apartment. Nora Hilton said in her note that she'd get in touch with him today. If she has, maybe we can find out what we want to know from him."

But when I reached Barto's apartment and knocked at his door, there was no answer. Neither was there any sound from inside to indicate that he might be there.

Feeling a little discouraged over my repeated failures to find any of the people I was seeking, I returned to Deirdre in the car and reported to her this latest disappointment. As usual, she came up with an encouraging suggestion.

"Maybe Miss Hilton got in touch with him by letter," she offered. "Has he got a mailbox in the dormitory reception room?"

"No," I answered. "Mail for faculty members is taken up to their rooms and slipped under the door. But I couldn't tamper with his mail, Derry; that's a Federal offense."

"Of course you couldn't," she agreed. "But you could find out whether such a letter arrived from the name and return address on the envelope. Why don't you ask Dr. Prentiss whether he couldn't let you into Professor Barto's apartment just long enough to make sure? I'm positive he'd go along with you himself to help you."

Knowing Prentiss, I was inclined to agree with her on that. In fact, I would have gone even further and predicted that if I went at all, he would accompany me.

I left her then, and went around to his office in College Hall.

He appeared slightly scandalized when I told him my story, but I couldn't be sure whether it was because I wanted to go into Barto's rooms during his absence and examine his mail or because he'd just learned that the head of his dramatics department was involved in some campus intrigue, if not worse. However, he agreed to grant my request and, as I had anticipated, to go with me.

"Although it is highly irregular to enter the room of a faculty member during his absence and without his permission," he reminded me, "I believe that such a procedure would be warranted in this particular instance. I'm glad, Laing, that you had the prudence to come to me in this matter, instead of simply asking the house superintendent to unlock the door and examine Professor Barto's letters for you."

He accompanied me back to the men's dormitory then; and after he had obtained the pass-key from the superintendent, we went up to Barto's apartment and he unlocked the door.

"My sacred word!" he exclaimed almost the instant he had stepped across the threshold. "This is a most unusual room for a university professor! There are more pictures of—what is the term?—pin-up girls decorating his walls than you'd be liable to find in a whole hall of undergraduates. But that is no more than is to be expected of a man of Barto's background, I suppose. You see, Laing, he wasn't always a member of the teaching profession. He used to be an actual theatrical director on Broadway—or just off it. And I believe at one time he went to Hollywood to do some work in pictures, also." He made the last sound like some sort of slumming expedition.

He crossed to one of the walls for the apparent pur-

pose of examining the photographs, while I waited with
what patience I could muster for him to return to the
original business that had brought us there.

"Here are pictures of Ethel Barrymore, Estelle Tay-
lor, Helen Hayes, and a host of equally famous ladies
of the theater," he observed with an interest that would
probably have surprised many of his students. "Some
of them even bear personal inscriptions. And here," he
paused almost reverently, "is a picture of Helena Stedman. I wonder whether he knew her personally, too."

"Is there no inscription on the picture?" I inquired.

"Not unless it's on the back," he replied. "And since
he has it in a silver frame on his desk, I feel that I've
no right to examine it to find out." He turned away
from it, and I fancied I heard him breathe a faint sigh,
as if in tribute to the vanished snows of yesteryear.

"But now as to that letter you're interested in." He
dragged himself back to the present, and came over to
the door beside which I had remained standing. Then
he stooped, and I heard him pick up several pieces of
mail from the floor.

"A copy of *Billboard*," he murmured as he examined
them, "an advertisement from a play-publishing house,
what looks like a bill from a ladies' apparel shop," his
voice had raised eyebrows over that one, "and a notice
from the library that he has a book overdrawn. I'm
afraid the letter you're interested in isn't here, Laing."

"Foiled again!" I exclaimed lightly to cover up my
real disappointment.

"Perhaps this Miss Hilton—or Mrs. Fordyce, as she probably is by this time—will attempt to communicate with Barto by telephone," he suggested as he relocked the door. "If she should do so before he returns, I'll instruct the switchboard operator to transfer the call to my office. Since this is a police matter, inasmuch as young Fordyce is wanted by them for questioning in connection with his father's death, I feel that we are justified in resorting to somewhat—er—unusual tactics."

I began to suspect that Prentiss possessed potentialities I'd never even dreamed of.

He went back to his office then, and I returned home. When I got there, I found that Mark had come back.

CHAPTER IX

Deirdre met me on the porch with the news. "And, Paddy, he isn't married," she finished. "I don't know whether to be glad or sorry."

"You mean glad for Lee's sake or sorry because of the alibi?" I inquired.

"Yes," she answered soberly. "Of course, it may still be all right about the alibi, I'm not sure. But you'd better get him to tell you about it himself."

I went into the house, where she told me the boy was waiting for me. I found him in the living room with Lee, whose attitude toward him seemed to be an odd mixture of sympathetic solicitude and formal reserve; the latter, I had no doubt, being the result of the abortive marriage episode, which she had learned about by this time.

"Remember your promise, Pat," were her first words to me as I came into the room. Then she tactfully went out onto the porch to join Deirdre so that Mark could tell me his story without the embarrassment of her presence.

"I guess I'd better start at the point where Dad and I

got back from the theater," he began as soon as we were alone. His voice was steady and well under control, but I suspected that he was keeping it so only by a determined effort. "When we got back to the house, we had a terrific fight—I'll not attempt to deny that. I'd never seen him so angry before, and I couldn't understand the reason for it. I'd done something I'd known he wouldn't approve of, it was true; but I hadn't committed any crime, yet he behaved almost as if I had. I told him so, and I'll never forget the look he gave me. Then he told me I'd committed more than a crime, that I'd sinned against him and against myself, and that the theater was nothing but a den of harlots and lecherers.

"That was a little stronger language than I was willing to take, even from him, and I said that if that was the way he felt about it, I'd better get out. I went up to my room, threw some things into a suitcase, and slammed out of the house without even saying goodbye to him."

His voice trembled a little over the last words, as though the memory they evoked brought with it a poignant regret that would take a long time to heal.

"Was that when you went to meet Nora Hilton?" I asked to help get him over the bad spot.

"It was when I met her," he replied, "although we hadn't planned the meeting. When I left the house, I'd intended to go over to Professor Barto's apartment, and ask him if I could spend the night with him. I hadn't any definite plan in mind for the immediate future, and

I thought maybe he could help me work out one. Then as I was cutting across campus, I ran into Nora.

"I told her what had happened—about the fight I'd had with Dad, I mean; she already knew what had taken place at the theater—and she was sympathetic. She always had a way of saying just the things I wanted to hear, and she said them then. I don't know exactly how it happened after that, but before I realized what I was doing, I'd asked her to marry me.

"She told me she would; then she suggested that we drive across the state line where we could have the ceremony performed right away instead of waiting the three days required in this state to get a license. She said she knew of a car we could borrow, since of course I couldn't take my father's car.

"That wasn't exactly the way I'd thought about doing it, but it sounded like a good idea, and I agreed. She told me then to wait for her at the entrance to the campus while she went to borrow the car."

"At what time was this?" I inquired, mindful of his alibi.

"A few minutes past eleven o'clock," he answered, "shortly after you and Mrs. Laing and Lee—" He stopped awkwardly.

"Yes, I remember." I glossed over the incident of the encounter in front of the Fine Arts Building as though it had been of no consequence. "And she came back with the car?"

"Yes. She was gone about five minutes—maybe ten

at the outside—then she drove up in a DeSoto sedan that she explained belonged to a friend of hers. I asked her whether she'd told her friend what she wanted the car for. She answered that she had, and laughed in a queer way I didn't understand at the time, and which I still don't."

He paused momentarily, as though the memory of it continued to puzzle him, then continued:

"We drove around to her boarding house first, and I waited in the car while she went up to her room and packed a week-end bag; then we started off again.

"We drove for about an hour without either of us saying very much. I didn't feel like talking—I was still bothered about that fight I'd had with Dad—and she acted as if she had private matters on her mind. All of a sudden she brought the car to a stop—she'd been doing the driving—and turned sideways in the seat to face me. She looked at me for a minute as if she were studying me, then said, 'Look here, kid; you don't really want to get married, do you?' And believe it or not, Professor Laing, as soon as she'd said it, I realized that I didn't.

"But of course I couldn't admit that to her—it would hardly have been the decent thing to do—so I pretended to put up an argument. She let me speak my little piece, and it must have sounded pretty silly to her. I know it did to me. When I'd finished it, she said almost as though she were pitying me, 'Listen, Mark, you're not in love with me, and what's more, I'm not in love with you. All you wanted tonight was somebody's shoulder to cry on, and mine happened to be handy; while all I wanted was to finish a job I'd been hired to do. Well, I've finished it now, or as much of it as I intend to finish, and I'm going back to New York. As for you, there'll be another shoulder you can do your crying on. They say women are like streetcars, you know: if the first one won't stop for you, there'll be another one along in a few minutes.'

"I'd never heard her talk like that before, kind of hard, and—well, almost cheap; and it bothered me. It gave me the feeling I'd been made a fool of in some way, but I wasn't sure just how. I asked her what she'd meant by that part about wanting to finish a job she'd been hired to do, but she refused to tell me. Then she laughed the way she had back there at the entrance to the campus when I'd asked her if her friend knew why she wanted the car, and said that if I ever did find out, she hoped she and another certain party she could name would be miles away at the time.

"That made me more certain than ever that I'd been taken for some kind of a sucker ride, and I started to get mad. I asked her if she'd changed her mind about marrying me because she'd begun to realize I wasn't a very good prospect now that I'd broken off with my father. That made *her* mad, and she answered that if I thought I was a prize catch either with or without my father, I'd better go off in a corner somewhere and take stock of myself. It ended with my getting out of the car and walking off, while she drove on."

At any other time I would have been amused by the idea of the boy's walking home from the ride instead of the girl. Just then, however, I saw nothing humorous in the situation.

"What time was it when you left her?" I asked.

"About one o'clock, I think," he answered, and I breathed a sigh of relief. If he had been in the company of Nora Hilton until one o'clock, his alibi was safe.

"We'd been out in the middle of nowhere when she stopped the car," he went on after a moment, "and I had to walk nearly five miles along a deserted country road before I reached the nearest town. It turned out to be a little jerk-water place that wasn't much more than a whistle-stop so far as the railroads were concerned, and I had to wait until four o'clock in the morning before I was able to get a train home.

"By the time I got here, I was feeling pretty sick of the whole night's performance and everything connected with it—myself included. I was also feeling a little ashamed of the way I'd walked out on Dad, for I guessed he hadn't meant half of what he'd said any more than I had. I decided to go home and admit to him what a damned fool I'd made of myself, and tell him I was sorry; but first I knew I'd have to get a couple minutes' rest or I wouldn't be able to make it as far as the bus line. I'd had to stand all the way on the train, because it was crowded with a bunch of Elks or something on their way home from a convention, and I was practically out on my feet.

"I went over to a corner of the waiting room and found a seat. I hadn't meant to go to sleep or even to close my eyes, but that's what I must have done almost the minute I sat down. Nobody bothered me, and I didn't get awake until this afternoon.

"When I finally opened my eyes, I found that I'd been sitting opposite a newsstand. And there on one of the papers facing me was a big black headline telling how Dad—"

His voice broke on that, and he couldn't go on.

I went over to him and placed my hand on his shoulder without saying anything. There isn't much that can be said at such a time.

I waited until I was sure he had gained control of himself; then I asked, "And you came out here immediately after that?"

"I stopped to buy one of the papers and read the story first," he replied. "But tell me, Professor Laing, why do the police want to question me about what happened to Dad? I wasn't even here at the time."

I explained as tactfully as I could, for I felt that the boy had enough to bear already. Even at that, I couldn't soften the hard fact that he was under suspicion of his father's murder.

"My God!" he cried in horror when understanding of this had finally broken upon him. "They certainly can't believe that I— Why, I loved my father, Professor Laing! I'd never have harmed a hair on his head, even when we were having that quarrel."

"I know that, Mark," I told him, "and I said so to Lieutenant McDermott, who happens to be a friend of mine. I feel certain he'll believe it once he's talked to you."

He sprang up from the sofa where he had been sitting. "Then I've got to see him right away!" he exclaimed. "We've got to straighten this out, so he can start looking for the person who really did kill my dad. Will you go along with me?"

I told him that I would.

CHAPTER X

We found McDermott waiting for us in his private office, for I had telephoned him before leaving the house that we were coming. He listened to Mark's story almost in silence, interrupting only to ask the same questions about time that I had asked.

After it was finished, he remained silent for several seconds, as though he were thinking over what he had just heard. At last he spoke.

"Granting you had nothing to do with your father's murder," he began, "what's your own theory as to how it might have happened? Did he have any enemies that you know of?"

"No," Mark answered. "Dad was always a reserved sort, never making many close friends or any enemies. So far as I'm aware, there wasn't anybody who knew him well enough to have what they might have thought was a reason for killing him."

"Yet somebody did kill him," McDermott pointed out tersely.

Mark hesitated before offering a reply to this; then he said slowly:

"There's only one possibility I can think of, Lieutenant. Dad and Professor Fosdick out at the university were working on some kind of a chemical experiment. I don't know what it was about, because he never told me and I was never sufficiently interested to ask, but I know that it was something for the Government. Maybe this sounds a little melodramatic, but if the thing they were working on was sufficiently important, isn't it possible that a spy from some foreign government might have killed Dad to get it?"

McDermott merely grunted without committing himself. He turned abruptly to the young policeman who had been taking down the interview in shorthand.

"Get me that package from the other room, Evans," he directed: "the one wrapped in brown paper."

The policeman went to do as he was bidden. In a moment he came back with something which he laid on the desk in front of McDermott.

There followed the rustle of paper as the lieutenant unwrapped it, but I had no way of knowing what it was until he spoke.

"Ever see this hat before, Fordyce?" he inquired almost casually.

Mark bent forward to examine it. "No, not that I can remember," he said then. "It's not one of my father's, if that's what you had in mind."

"Try it on," McDermott suggested.

There was a brief interval of silence; then he spoke again.

"No, I guess not," he decided. "Even a college boy wouldn't be seen in a hat that comes down over his ears the way that one does on you."

"You thought it was mine?" Mark asked in surprise.

"Your initials are stamped on the inside," McDermott pointed out. "Or do you know of somebody else who's got those same initials?"

Mark admitted that he did not.

McDermott gave the hat back to the policeman to take away again.

"I ought to keep you here, Fordyce, until this Hilton woman can be found to corroborate your story," he said then. "But instead of doing that, I'm going to give you a break. If Professor Laing will be responsible for you and agree to have you here the next time I want you, and if you'll give me your word not to try to run out on him, I'll turn you loose. Is it a deal?"

"You don't believe my story, then?" Mark asked, disappointed.

McDermott softened a trifle. "It's not a question of whether I believe it or not, son," he explained. "It's a question of whether you can prove it. I'm just a cop with a job to do, and certain rules to govern the way I do it. One of them says I can't go by whether or not I *think* a man's telling the truth; I've got to go by the evidence. But we haven't got any evidence except your unsupported word that you were with the Hilton woman last night at the time your father was killed, and we won't have until she turns up. However, I think we may be able to find her for you if you'll give us her description."

Mark furnished the description, which the policeman, Evans, took down.

"Take that up to the boys in the teletype room, and tell them to send it out right away," McDermott directed him. "We can't have her picked up, because there's nothing we can charge her with, but we can at least try to locate her. You can give that description to the newspapers, too," he added as an afterthought. "But make it clear that the girl isn't wanted for anything except to prove or disprove Fordyce's alibi. We don't want her to get scared and go into hiding on us."

He turned back to Mark. "You can run along now, son," he said. "If you're telling the truth—and I'll admit I've a notion that you are—you've got nothing to worry about."

I sent Mark on home alone while I remained behind with McDermott, for I wanted to tell him what I had learned a few hours earlier from Nora Hilton's roommate, Hazel Phipps, concerning Barto.

"I don't know how or where he enters into this," I concluded, "or for that matter, whether he enters into it at all. But it seems odd that Nora Hilton should have mentioned in that note she left for her roommate that if Barto called, he was to be told she'd get in touch with him the next day."

"I agree with you," McDermott said thoughtfully. "It's one of those things that add up to zero. All we have is that the Hilton woman was a friend of this Barto's, and that she left word for her roommate to tell him she'd get in touch with him after she was married to Mark. Nothing in that to connect either one of them with the murder, and yet . . ."

He leaned back in his chair, which groaned protestingly under his weight. "Of course, there's the possibility that the postscript had nothing to do with the rest of the note, but I've a hunch it did. Pat, I've a notion to go see this Phipps girl myself, and find out if she can tell me anything more. Want to go with me? She may talk more freely with you along, since she already knows you."

But Hazel Phipps was unable to add anything to what she had already told me. She was a little resentful at first when she learned McDermott was a detective, but she unbent again when she found he was interested in Nora Hilton only in connection with Mark's alibi. She even, at his suggestion, managed to find him a snapshot of Nora Hilton.

"I took this myself a little over a month ago," she said as she gave it to him. "Nora's the one on the right. The other girl's Dixie. She's a blonde who lives on the second floor."

McDermott thanked him and pocketed the picture, also the note which Nora Hilton had written. Then we rose to leave.

We had got as far as the front steps when the girl, who had accompanied us to the door, suddenly stopped us.

"Wait a minute!" she exclaimed. "I've just thought of something! It won't help you to find Nora, but since in a way it concerns Tony Barto and since you seem to be as interested in him as you are in her, maybe I'd better tell it to you anyway."

McDermott turned at once. "What is it, Miss Phipps?" he demanded. "Anything that concerns Barto may be important."

"It happened about two months ago," she began, dropping her voice to a conspiratorial whisper. "Nora had been out on a date with Mark Fordyce that evening—it was only about the second or third real date they'd had.

"After she got back, she was sitting in front of the dressing table brushing her hair before going to bed, when all of a sudden she began to laugh. I asked her what was so funny, and she said, 'I was just thinking, Haze: When I first came here Tony Barto told me something that I certainly could raise some merry hell with if I ever decided to double-cross him and repeated it in certain quarters.' I asked her whether it had anything to do with Mark, knowing she'd just been out with him; and she laughed again and said, 'I'll say it does, and how!'

"I asked her what it was, but she wouldn't tell me. All she'd say was, 'I should tell you, and then maybe have you turn around and use it to blackmail—' "

She broke off in confusion, as though she had just remembered that she was talking to a police officer.

McDermott pretended not to have noticed the slip. "Did she say who the person was she was afraid you might repeat the story to?" he inquired diplomatically.

"No, she didn't," Miss Phipps answered, evidently both relieved and reassured by his choice of words. "All she said was, 'One of the parties concerned.' Maybe she meant Tony; I don't know. But I'm pretty sure from the way she said it, she didn't mean Mark."

Since she had nothing further to add to her story, McDermott thanked her for the information she had given us, and this time we actually did leave.

"Now I'm going to run out to the university and see whether your Professor Antonio Barto's come back yet," McDermott said as we drove away from the boarding house. "It may be just a coincidence that he didn't show up for his classes the morning after Dr. Fordyce was murdered; but if he's definitely skipped out, it's a sure sign he knows something he's trying to hide. And whatever it is, I'm going to find him and sweat it out of him if I've got to."

I didn't accompany him on his quest for Barto. After all, the man was an associate of mine at the university; and I felt that the lieutenant could handle him with more freedom—also that Barto himself would respond with less restraint—if I wasn't present during the interview.

When I returned home, I found Mark arrived ahead of me. Deirdre had insisted that he remain with us for the present at least, since to have gone back to his own home next door would have been too painful for him.

I had gone upstairs to brush up before dinner when it suddenly occurred to me that Mark himself might be able to furnish some further information concerning the relationship that existed between Barto and the woman, Nora Hilton. I hurried down again, and was relieved to find him alone in the living room; Lee, who had been with him before, having gone to the kitchen to assist Deirdre with the preparation of dinner.

"Mark," I began when I had taken a chair opposite him, "there are some questions I'd like to ask you about Miss Hilton. Do you feel up to answering them just now?"

"No reason why not," he answered with a short laugh that had no mirth behind it. "She isn't exactly one of my favorite topics, but I'd as soon discuss her as a number of other things I could mention. What is it you'd like to know about her?"

"Suppose you begin with how you first came to meet her," I suggested.

"It was through Professor Barto," he replied. "He'd brought her with him to a meeting of the Drama Club about three months ago, and introduced her to us fellows as an actress friend of his from New York, who was here resting between plays. Most of us had never met a real actress before, and we were—I suppose 'intrigued' is the word. For some reason she seemed to become interested in me right from the start, and we spent nearly half the evening off in a corner by our-

selves discussing theater. Just before she left, I took my
nerve in my hands and asked her if I could see her
again before long. She told me I could, and from then
on . . ." He left the rest of it to my imagination.

"Have you any idea why she should have become so
interested in you?" I inquired.

"I thought it was because Professor Barto must have
told her I wanted to become an actor, and I was con-
ceited enough to believe she felt I had talent." He gave
another of those short, humorless laughs, as if in self-
mockery. "I remember she became highly indignant
when I told her Dad was opposed to my having a stage
career, and she asked me whether I'd ever considered
going on with it without his consent. I admitted I had
toyed with the idea once or twice, and right away she
started to encourage me in it. She said that with a talent
as great as mine," a note of self-conscious embarrassment crept into his voice, "no one had the right to stand
in my way, not even my own father; that to keep me
away from the stage would be to deny me my natural
birthright."

Memory of Barto's words to me that day in the
restaurant flitted across my mind. This speech of Nora
Hilton's to Mark sounded as though it might well have
been an echo of them.

"She used to ask me a lot of questions about Dad,"
the boy went on: "What sort of man he was, whether
he'd ever given me any hint as to why he was so opposed to my going into the theater, and so on. I ad-

mitted that he never had, since he'd always refused to discuss the subject with me when I brought it up."

"Did she ever tell you why she should have asked these questions about your father?" I inquired.

"No," he answered, "but I supposed it was just natural curiosity about him because of her interest in me. I did get an odd feeling, though, once or twice," he paused, as though trying to materialize a nebulous impression, "that she was asking for another reason—as if she knew something about Dad that I didn't, and was interested in him because of that. But that's ridiculous, of course."

I wasn't so sure that it was.

"Did she ever talk to you about Professor Barto?" I asked next. "What her association had been with him in the past, or how she had happened to renew their former acquaintance after coming here?"

"No," he answered again. "So far as I can remember, we never discussed Professor Barto."

I let the subject drop then, for it was plain that he could tell me nothing further. One piece of information he had given us, however, stood out in my mind as being of undoubted significance: Nora Hilton had expressed a marked interest in Dr. Eric Fordyce, an interest, I was practically certain, which had its origin in something she had learned about him from Antonio Barto.

The pieces of the puzzle were beginning, if not actually to fit together, at least to indicate a definite relationship to one another.

CHAPTER XI

That evening around nine o'clock, McDermott rang me up on the telephone.

"It's beginning to look more and more as though your friend Barto's skipped out on us, Pat," he announced. "He wasn't in his rooms at the dormitory when I went there this afternoon, and as far as the house superintendent and the telephone operator knew, he hadn't been there all day, so I started making inquiries about him. I found out among other things that he keeps his car at a garage a couple of blocks from the university; but when I went there to check on it, one of the garage attendants told me Barto had taken it out last night shortly after eleven o'clock, and never brought it back. So it looks as if our bird has flown."

"Hold on a minute, Mac," I put in. "I think I know what became of the car. I believe it's the one Nora Hilton told Mark last night she'd borrowed from a friend. The coincidence of the time involved is almost too great for it to be otherwise."

"Damned if I don't believe you're right!" he exclaimed after a moment's reflection. "Then if we can find the car, we'll probably find the Hilton woman at the same time, or at least get a line on her. I'm going to send out a seven-state alarm for it over both the radio and the teletype just as soon as I can get its description and license number from that garage where he kept it. But that still doesn't tell us what's become of Barto. Did she pick him up in it after she'd ditched Mark Fordyce, or did she turn it back to him to go off in by himself?"

"I'm afraid you'll have to wait until you've found her to get the answers to those questions," I told him.

"Blast it all!" he exclaimed impatiently. "There are getting to be too many questions we've got to wait to get the answers to until we've found her! I'm beginning to suspect that this woman, Nora Hilton, may be the key to the whole mystery."

I wasn't willing to go along with him quite so far as that, but I did suspect that Nora Hilton, when and if she was found, would be able to give us information that would tell us where to look for the key and how to use it when we'd found it.

"Another thing," he added just before he rang off: "Acting on that suggestion young Mark made back in my office this afternoon, I went around to see this Professor Fosdick about the work he and Dr. Fordyce had been doing for the Government; but he was close-mouthed as a clam. He admitted they'd been working on some chemical formula, but that was as far as he'd go. I couldn't decide whether he's just a little man trying to appear important, or whether he's a really important one who's being extra cautious. I'm going to phone Washington long-distance in the morning, and see what they've got to say on the subject. If this whole thing should have any sort of international angle, they ought to know about it in any case."

I thought that of the two possibilities he had mentioned concerning Fosdick, the former was the more likely. Fosdick was, I knew, the sort of man who considered any activity with which he happened to be associated of major importance.

I was still turning the possibilities over in my mind when I went to sleep that night, but without having arrived at any conclusion which completely satisfied me.

It was somewhere in the neighborhood of two o'clock in the morning when Deirdre awakened me.

"Get up, Paddy," she commanded. "I want you to find out whether Mark's in his room."

"Why shouldn't he be?" I asked drowsily. "The boy's probably still exhausted from not having had any sleep last night."

"I'll tell you why he might not be," she replied, continuing to shake me by the shoulder: "Because there's a light next door in the Fordyce house, in the room that was Dr. Fordyce's study."

That brought me wide awake in a hurry.

"Good Lord!" I exclaimed, and sprang out of bed as though it had suddenly turned into a bed of hot coals. "If he *has* gone over there for any reason and the police catch him there, they may think . . ."

I raced down the hall to the guest room, which Mark was occupying. But at the door I paused and stood listening for a moment. If the boy was in bed and asleep, I had no wish to rush in and waken him needlessly. However, I could hear no sound of regular breathing from the other side of the door to tell me he was there.

I went into the room then and crossed to the bed. Although the bedclothes had been disturbed, my hand encountered no sleeping figure beneath them.

Returning to Deirdre, I told her of my discovery. "I'm going over there and bring him back," I finished. "He's under suspicion as it is; if he's discovered poking about his father's study under circumstances that it might be difficult to explain, it will only add to that suspicion."

"Then I'm going with you," Deirdre announced. "There was a policeman on duty there this afternoon. He may still be somewhere around; and if he is, I can help you keep clear of him."

I didn't argue the point with her, although I'd have preferred that she remain where she was. There was the barest chance that the man whose light she had seen might not be Mark Fordyce after all.

Five minutes later, we were making our way across the silent lawn to the house next door.

As we crossed the porch to the front door, the thought crossed my mind that Mark might have locked it behind him. But my misgivings were short-lived; it was not only unlocked, but standing slightly ajar.

We pushed it cautiously wider and stepped into the little entry hall beyond. Both it and the living room which it gave were deserted, but a robust snore issuing from the direction of the dining room told us the whereabouts of the policeman who had been left on duty to guard the premises.

With Deirdre leading the way, we crossed the living room and started up the stairs. The seventh one let out a loud creak as she trod on it, and we heard the snores in the dining room go into a kind of momentary convulsion during which I think both our hearts skipped a beat; but the sleeper didn't waken.

"Keep as close to the wall as you can, Derry," I whispered. "The boards are less likely to be loose on that side."

She followed my advice, and, feeling a little like common criminals on the one hand and musical comedy conspirators on the other, we made the rest of the ascent without further mishap.

When we had reached the second floor hall, we paused a moment while Deirdre peered down it to where she reported the door to Dr. Fordyce's study was standing open at its far end.

"He's sitting in the chair in front of his father's desk," she said into my ear. "You'd better speak to him when we reach the doorway, Paddy. If we come up too close behind him before he knows we're there, it may startle him."

I nodded, and took the lead as we proceeded down the hall. When I felt the lintel of the study doorway under my hand, I spoke.

"Mark," I began, keeping my voice lowered so that it would reach no farther than the man for whom it was intended, "you shouldn't—"

I was interrupted by a startled vociferation and the sound of a chair going over backwards as the man who had been occupying it leaped to his feet.

"Heavens!" Deirdre gasped. "It isn't Mark at all!"

"Fosdick!" I exclaimed, recognizing his voice. "What in the world are you doing here?"

Before he could answer, there came the thump of heavy footsteps pounding up the stairs, and the policeman was upon us.

"What's goin' on here?" he demanded in the voice of authority. "Who are all you people, and just what do ye think you're doin'?"

"It's all right, Officer," I assured him, and hoped secretly that it would turn out that way. "My name is Patrick Laing. My wife, here, thought she saw a light over here from our house next door; and since I'm working unofficially with Lieutenant McDermott on this case, we thought we'd better come over and investigate."

There was a brief silence while he looked us over.

"I guess ye're tellin' the truth," he finally admitted grudgingly, "seein' as how ye've only got your pants on over your nightclothes, although by rights I ought to hold ye here while I send for the lieutenant to come out and identify ye, just to be on the safe side. But who's this little guy?" I knew he was staring at Fosdick.

"I am Mortimer Fosdick," the "little guy" answered for himself. "Professor of inorganic chemistry at the university."

"Alcatraz University, more likely," the policeman snorted. "Don't ye know there's a law against breaking and entering, or doesn't it make any difference to ye?"

"I didn't *break* and enter," Fosdick denied indignantly. "I merely entered through the front door, which I found unlocked. There is a legal difference."

"And it's a lucky thing for you that there is," the policeman told him, "or I'd be runnin' ye down to the calaboose to think over your sins. Maybe I ought to do it anyway if ye haven't got a good explanation for what ye were doin' here," he added undecidedly.

Fosdick hesitated. "Since you are an officer of the law," he said finally, "I suppose it will be safe to tell you. I came here tonight to look for certain notes of Dr. Fordyce's on an experiment which we have been conducting jointly for the United States Government. But I refuse to give you any information as to the nature of the experiment," he finished with a flash of defiance.

"I'll vouch for Professor Fosdick, Officer," I put in. "He probably didn't inform you of the purpose of his visit upon his arrival, because he didn't want to waken you. However, if you have any further doubts about him, you can check with Lieutenant McDermott."

I don't know whether it was my free use of McDermott's name or my reference to his having been asleep while on duty that did the trick, but he unexpectedly relented.

"If you're sure he's okay, Mr. Laing, I guess I can take a chance on him," he said with less hostility in his voice. "But he's got a bad eye, and I don't like it."

He escorted the three of us down to the front door then, and I'm positive stood there looking after us until Deirdre and I had reached ours.

As we were about to say good night to Fosdick at the entrance to our front walk, there came the sound of footsteps approaching from the opposite direction. Against the surrounding stillness of the night, they sounded oddly hollow and lonely.

"Why, it's Mark!" Deirdre exclaimed. Her tone betrayed that she had completely forgotten that we had gone out originally in search of him.

"I couldn't sleep, so I dressed and went for a walk," Mark explained apologetically as he came up to us. "I hope you haven't been worried about me."

Deirdre, whose sense of humor not infrequently gets the better of her, told him of our night's adventure, and I'm afraid unconsciously laid it on to Fosdick a little.

"I very much fear that the amusing side of the incident failed to penetrate my consciousness," the chemistry professor observed somewhat stiffly when she had finished. "The safe recovery of those notes before they fall into the wrong hands is a most vital matter. I would greatly appreciate it, Mark, if you could find an opportunity to assist me with the problem."

Mark's reply must have been a disappointment to him.

"I'm afraid that's something I can't do, Professor," the boy said flatly. "In the first place, I wouldn't know a simple chemistry formula from a gas meter reading. But even if I did, I doubt that the police would permit me to remove anything from Dad's study just now."

We said good night to Fosdick and were about to part company with him when Mark spoke to him again.

"Professor Fosdick," he asked, "would you mind telling me your first and middle names?"

Fosdick paused. "I don't know why the subject should interest you," he retorted, and his tone implied that he also didn't know what concern it was of Mark's, "but my first name is Mortimer. I have no middle name that I care to use." Then he walked rapidly away.

"Why *did* it interest you, Mark?" I inquired as we entered the house.

"Just an idea that flashed through my mind," he answered. "I was thinking of the initials inside that hat."

CHAPTER XII

The following morning, Deirdre told me, the newspapers all carried reproductions of the snapshot of Nora
Hilton which Hazel Phipps had given to McDermott,
topped with the caption, "Has Anyone Seen This
Woman?" The stories that followed could tell little
other than that she was being sought to corroborate
Mark Fordyce's account of his whereabouts at the time
his father was killed, but they hinted almost without
exception that she might have some closer connection
with the case which the police were keeping under
cover until she should be found.

Although McDermott had given out both the picture
and the information that the woman was wanted in the
hope that the publicity might prove helpful in locating
her, the way the matter had been handled by the reporters threatened to defeat this purpose; for if, as the
lieutenant and I were coming to believe, she was more
deeply concerned in the mystery than appeared upon
the surface, these stories would put her on her guard
and possibly even send her into hiding. They were also,
from my standpoint, unfortunate in another way; for

by connecting her name with that of Mark Fordyce,
they gave the first public intimation that he might be
suspect in his father's murder.

I had little time, however, to speculate upon the possible results of this blundering by the press, for at ten
o'clock the inquest into the death of Dr. Eric Fordyce
was held.

It was conducted in a police school lecture room at
City Hall, with only the coroner's jury, the known
principals in the case, and, of course, the reporters permitted to be present. Mark and the firemen who had
discovered the body were the only witnesses called upon
to testify.

I was relieved when the boy was asked no questions
concerning the quarrel with his father, but only about
the time he had last seen him alive and whether or not
Dr. Fordyce had mentioned that he was expecting any
visitors later that night. At least the newspapers would
not have that to serve up in their columns, garnished
with the usual damaging innuendoes. But I realized that
in all probability it would not be long before they dug
up that incident of the rehearsal for themselves, and
then more mischief would be afoot.

When the inquest was finally over and the usual verdict of "Death at the hands of some person unknown"
had been handed down and written into the record, I
remained for a word with McDermott in his private
office.

"I suppose there's been no trace yet of either Nora Hilton or Barto?" I asked him.

"Not a trace," he answered. "After Barto took his car out of the garage night before last, and after the Hilton woman let young Fordyce out of it somewhere and drove away a couple of hours later, both of them seem to have dropped completely out of sight.

"I did pick up a little additional information on Barto, however," he went on, "although it doesn't help any insofar as locating him's concerned. I questioned the telephone operator who's on duty evenings at the men's dormitory where he lives, and she told me that just as she was about to go off duty that night, a call came in for him; and since it was in a woman's voice, she admits she listened in.

"She says Barto sounded as if he was in a bad humor when he first answered, but when he found out who was calling, he sweetened up a little. The woman said, 'Tony, this is Nora. Can I borrow your car for tonight?' He asked her what she wanted with it, and she answered, 'Believe it or not, Tony, I'm going to be married, and I'll give you three guesses who to.'

"According to the operator, he exclaimed something in Spanish that didn't sound as though he was exactly pleased with what she'd just told him, then said, 'Look here, Nora, I hadn't expected you to go quite as far as that.' The woman laughed and asked, 'Exactly how far were you expecting me to go? Or is it just that I'm going about it in the wrong way?'

"Barto called her what the operator described as a five letter word beginning with B and ending with H. She says she thought sure the woman would get mad, but that instead, she only laughed again and remarked that at least she was being called one by an expert on the subject. That made Barto mad, and he told her that if she wasn't careful, he'd spike her guns for her by not letting her have the car. Then just as quickly he cooled down again and said, as nearly as the operator could remember, 'On second thought, Nora, I begin to like your plans, although I don't imagine that the good Dr. Fordyce will when he finds out. Wait for me in front of the corner drug store. I'll be there in five minutes.' Then he rang off.

"He came running down the stairs and went out of the building while the operator was still putting on her hat; and except for the garage attendant a few minutes later, that seems to be the last anybody saw of him."

He took time out to light a cigarette; then he concluded, "At least we know for certain now that there's some definite connection between the Hilton woman and Barto which involves Mark Fordyce and possibly his father, judging from that single reference the telephone operator heard him make to Dr. Fordyce. But the question still remains: Is there any connection between them and the murder?"

I realized what he meant: Although we had proved

that some sort of intrigue did exist of which Barto was apparently the instigator and Mark Fordyce the victim or at least the object, we had no proof that there was any link between it and what had happened at Dr. Fordyce's laboratory two nights before. For any evidence we had to the contrary, the two events might have been entirely unrelated.

"There's a little something concerning Nora Hilton that I learned from Mark yesterday after I got back from your office," I said, and told McDermott about the questions she had asked the boy concerning his father.

He puffed at his cigarette in silence for a few seconds after I had finished, then said slowly, "You know, Pat, the more I think about it, the more I wonder whether young Mark might not have hit the nail square on the head when he made that suggestion about the possibility of a spy ring's being involved in his father's murder. That would explain the Hilton woman's interest in Dr. Fordyce, and the impression the boy told you he'd got that she already knew something about his father. She may have been trying to pump him about this experiment."

"Possibly," I conceded, for that potentiality had already occurred to me. "But it doesn't explain why she should have been willing to marry Mark. Spies—even the Mata Haris of the profession—seldom go that far."

"Neither did she," he reminded me. "Don't forget

that according to Mark's story, she backed out at practically the last minute.

"Incidentally, I called Washington this morning, as I told you last night I was going to do," he went on. "They were pretty close-mouthed about the experiment; but when I told them the whole story and hinted that we had reason to believe the murder might be linked up with whatever it was Dr. Fordyce had been working on, they got interested and said they'd send a man up right away to look into matters. He's supposed to get here sometime this afternoon. Meanwhile, I've assigned two men of my own to backtrack on both Hilton and Barto, but so far they haven't had time to turn up anything."

Just then the telephone on his desk rang. He reached for it with a muttered exclamation of impatience, but the next minute his voice became crisp with excitement.

"What's that?" he barked. "Newark, New Jersey? . . You're blasted right I wanted to know. Give me that address again, so I can write it down. . . . Okay, I've got it. If the woman should come back before I can get there, stall her off, but try not to make her suspicious."

He flipped the telephone back upon its cradle.

"Pat, we've just had a break!" he announced jubilantly. "A garage operator in Newark picked up that description of Barto's car I had sent out on the police band of his radio, and he just now called to tell me he's got the car in his garage, and that a woman left it there early yesterday morning to have its engine gone over. I'm driving up there right away to get his story in detail, and if our luck holds, maybe to pick up Nora Hilton at the same time. Would you like to ride along?"

I told him with feeling that there was nothing I would like better.

CHAPTER XIII

I phoned Deirdre to tell her I wouldn't be home for lunch and to explain where I was going; then McDermott and I set out in a police car which he drove himself.

"I wish there was some charge I could have the Hilton woman held on until we could arrange to have her extradited in case she refuses to come back with us of her own accord," he remarked as we drove across the bridge into New Jersey. "But I haven't been able to think of a thing."

"What about material witness?" I suggested.

"Witness to what?" he asked ironically. "Not the murder. According to Mark Fordyce's story, she was miles away at the time. Yet I can't get the idea out of my head that she holds important information bearing on the case, if we only knew how to get it out of her. But since that's probably the reason why she ran away, she isn't likely to tell us of her own accord."

It took us close to two hours to complete the drive to Newark. When we got there, McDermott stopped to ask directions of a traffic policeman in the center of the city; then after another few minutes of driving, we arrived at our destination.

"This is it—Joe's Garage and Service Station," he announced, and swung the car in to the curb.

Joe himself came over to meet us as we climbed out. He was a young chap who smelled of an odd combination of car grease and hair oil.

"Is one of you gentlemen the Lieutenant McDermott I talked to over the telephone about that stolen car?" he asked eagerly, evidently having guessed our identity from our Pennsylvania license plates and from the police emblem on our own car.

"Yes, I am," McDermott answered. "But the car hasn't been stolen. We're tracing it for another reason. Is it still here?"

"You bet it's still here!" Joe replied. "Come inside and I'll show it to you."

We followed him into the garage.

"It's funny how I happened to find out about this car being wanted," he went on conversationally as he conducted us around several other cars that were parked on the floor. "I didn't get a chance to work on it until this morning; and while I did, I listened to the police calls over the radio like I always do, on account of the stolen car reports and me having a garage, you know.

"All of a sudden I realized one of the descriptions the fella was giving fitted the very car I was working on—'49 DeSoto sedan, light cream color with chocolate trim, Pennsylvania license. So I stopped what I was doing to the engine and waited for him to repeat it so I

could check the license number. And sure enough, it
checked. So I dropped everything and put in that call
to your police headquarters, and they connected me
with you."

"Good work," McDermott approved. "Is this the
car?"

"That's her, all right," Joe answered as all three of
us came to a stop.

McDermott walked around behind it to look at the
license plate. "It's the car we're looking for," he said
then. "Now I want to know all you can tell me about
the woman who brought it here. What time was it when
she came, what did she look like, and what did she say
to you?"

"It was somewhere around two o'clock Friday morning when she showed up," Joe replied, taking the questions in the order in which they had been put. "We've
got twenty-four hour service here, and I'd taken the
graveyard shift myself that night. Anyway, she drives
up in front of the gas pumps outside at about the time
I said, and honks her horn.

"I went out, thinking it was just a guy wanting gas.
Instead, I saw this good-lookin' dame all by herself in
the car. She wasn't no kid exactly, but she sure was a
fancy looker—big, dark eyes and dark, curly hair that
looked as if she'd just got done posing for a half of
those Which-Twin-Has-the-Toni ads. She was wearing
a little hat that wasn't much more than a bunch of

flowers perched on one side of her head, and she smelled like a million dollars.

"I asked her what I could do for her, and she asked me back if she could leave her car here to have the engine fixed. I said, 'Sure, lady. What seems to be the matter with it?' and she said, 'I don't know exactly, but after I've been driving for a while, it doesn't seem to run properly. Maybe you'd better give the engine a general overhauling.' I told her that might take a day or so, since I had some other jobs ahead of hers; and she answered that would be all right, since she was stopping in Newark over the week-end, and wouldn't be needing the car again until she was ready to leave.

"I got out my notebook and pencil then, and asked her for her name and the address of the place where she was stopping, so I could let her know when the job was finished. She sort of hesitated. Then she said her name was Catharine Bell and that she'd be stopping at the Hotel Newark, but that I shouldn't bother about calling, since she'd come and pick up the car some time Sunday when she was ready to leave, and did I think I could have it ready for her by then? I told her it would be ready; then she got out of the car, took one of those little week-end bags out of the back of it, and walked off down the street."

"And she hasn't come back since?" McDermott inquired.

"Not so's you could notice it," Joe answered. "But

then this is only Saturday, and she said she wouldn't be wanting the car before Sunday.

"It's a funny thing, though," he added as if the realization of it had not occurred to him until that very moment. "When I went to work on that car, I couldn't find a damned thing the matter with it."

McDermott and I didn't doubt that in the least.

"I'll send a man up either this evening or tomorrow morning to pick up the car," the lieutenant said as we got back into our own waiting car. "I'm sorry there's no reward offered for it, Joe, but if you'll send me the bill for that long distance telephone call you made to me about it, I'll see that it's taken care of."

Joe replied that he'd appreciate that. "But you mean the lady won't be back for the car herself?" he asked.

"Not if we catch up with her first, she won't," Mc-Dermott answered grimly.

The garage man whistled. "Gee!" he exclaimed. "To think of a classy-lookin' dame like that getting herself mixed up with the law!"

"I think now you've got your charge to hold Nora Hilton on if it becomes necessary," I remarked when we had driven away from the garage.

"Charge?" McDermott repeated. "What charge is that?"

"Car stealing," I replied. "Of course we know the car wasn't actually stolen, but she won't be able to prove that it wasn't, and it'll give you something to hold her on until you can find something better—or until you decide to let her go."

"Lord, that's so!" he exclaimed. "And for all she'll know, Barto could have made a charge against her. Funny that never occurred to me, even when Joe made that remark back there about the car's having been stolen. What with the way everybody's been appearing and disappearing in this case, I must be losing my grip."

We drove next to the Hotel Newark, where McDermott, after showing the desk clerk his police badge, inquired whether a Miss or Mrs. Catharine Bell had registered there early Friday morning.

There was a moment's delay while the clerk consulted the register.

"We've nobody staying here by that name," he reported then. "Sorry, Lieutenant."

"What about Nora Hilton, then?" McDermott inquired.

The clerk looked again. "Nor by that name, either," he replied.

McDermott made a third try. "Have you any woman between about thirty and thirty-five staying here?" he asked. "Dark eyes, brown curly hair, about five feet two inches tall and weighing around a hundred and twenty pounds."

"Oh, sure," the clerk answered. "There was one came in late Thursday afternoon, and another—" He stopped. "Say," he demanded excitedly, "isn't Nora Hilton the name of the woman who's wanted for questioning over in Pennsylvania in connection with the murder of some doctor last Thursday night?"

McDermott admitted that it was.

"I thought that name sounded familiar the minute you mentioned it," the clerk confided. "Like I was saying, we've got two or three women stopping here that her description would fit; but I saw her picture in the paper this morning, and she's not any of them."

We left the hotel in a state of disappointment that was all the keener because we had permitted our hopes to rise so high.

"I might have known our luck wouldn't hold," McDermott said in disgust. "It was all being just a little too easy. She probably took the first train out of Newark after leaving the car at the garage, and the Lord alone knows where she is by this time."

"My guess would be New York," I offered. "She told Mark that was where she was going, and we've no reason to suppose she might have changed her mind later, since Newark is on the way there."

"Unless she's definitely mixed up in the murder," he amended. "If she is, the place she said she was going would be the least likely place in the world where we'd be liable to find her.

"Just the same, I'll get in touch with the New York police, and ask them to help us locate her. We know that she was an actress and that she couldn't have had

too much money, since she was living at a cheap boarding house. That means she'll have to start looking for
work at the booking offices and casting agencies; and
when she does that, they ought to be able to spot her.

"But in the meantime," he added on a more gloomy
note, "Mark Fordyce is without a substantiated alibi
and the newspapers are without any other suspect in the
case. The combination isn't good."

CHAPTER XIV

It was only a little past three o'clock by the time Mc-Dermott and I returned from our little excursion into New Jersey, earlier than either of us had expected to get back. He went to his office then to await the arrival of the F. B. I. man he was expecting from Washington, while I returned home.

When I reached there I found Deirdre alone, Mark having gone to complete arrangements for his father's funeral.

"Lee went with him," she explained, "so I didn't offer to go along. I thought they'd prefer to be alone. But, Paddy, what's to become of that poor boy, now that his father's gone?"

"I believe he intends to complete his course at the university, seeing that he'll be graduated next month," I replied. "After that, if he's interested, I'll speak to Prentiss about the possibility of an instructorship in the dramatics department for him, since he probably won't be interested in going on the stage now. But he'll have to decide that for himself."

The thought crossed my mind as I said it that unless

Nora Hilton were found and found quickly, Mark might not be in a position to decide anything for himself. For no matter how much McDermott might be inclined personally to give him the benefit of the doubt, he was not, as he himself had pointed out the day before in his office, entirely unrestricted in his conduct of the case. The district attorney, for example, might decide that there was sufficient evidence against the boy to warrant his being charged with the murder and held for the grand jury, particularly if the newspapers began to stir up public opinion against him. In view of the story that had been in the morning editions, I was afraid they might do that at any minute. Furthermore, the hat which had been found in the ruins of the laboratory had been an exhibit at the inquest. It was almost inevitable that some enterprising reporter should fit those initials to Mark Fordyce's name.

Deirdre broke across my meditations with a question. "How was the trip to Newark?" she inquired. "Did the car turn out to be Professor Barto's?"

"Yes, it was Barto's, all right," I answered. "But that's the best that can be said for the whole trip." I told her then of our failure to locate Nora Hilton.

"You know, Paddy," she said when I had finished, "I've a hunch that when that girl finds out she's needed to substantiate Mark's alibi, she'll come back here of her own accord. Or she will if she's able to come back," she amended less optimistically.

"What's that supposed to mean?" I asked, not liking

the sound of it.

"I've been thinking while you were gone," she replied. "If there *is* a spy ring involved, as you say Lieutenant McDermott is beginning to think may be possible, and Nora Hilton and Professor Barto were mixed up in it, something may have happened to one or both of them. These head foreign agents often destroy their assistants to insure their silence once they have served their purpose and are no longer useful, don't they?"

I laughed and told her she had been listening to too many of the wrong kind of radio programs, but actually her suggestion had made me a little uneasy. That was all we needed, I thought, to insure Mark's being arrested immediately; to have it discovered that Nora Hilton had been murdered. For then he might find himself exonerated of one murder only to be accused of another—if not actually of both.

It was a little past five o'clock in the afternoon when McDermott, whom I had left barely two hours before, stopped by to see me. He was accompanied by a stranger whom he introduced as a Mr. Floyd Harbeson from the Federal Bureau of Investigation at Washington.

"It isn't that the work Dr. Fordyce and his colleague, Professor Fosdick, were engaged in was a particularly important secret," the F. B. I. man explained when the three of us had gone into my study. He was a quiet-spoken man whose manner suggested that he was one of those who could use words to conceal rather than to reveal his thoughts. (I had the feeling, as I listened to him, that he might be doing it now.) "Although naturally it is of some importance, otherwise it wouldn't be regarded as a secret in the first place." He laughed deprecatingly. "The thing that interests us at Washington is not so much whether it has been stolen as whether or not there actually is a ring of foreign agents operating in this locality; for if there is, they may have other irons in the fire—irons of a much more serious nature. That's what I've been sent up here to find out."

I told him that I understood his and the Government's position in the matter.

"At present I'm interested in the questions Lieutenant McDermott says young Fordyce told you this woman, Nora Hilton, asked him about his father, Professor Laing," he went on. "I'd like to know if any of them were concerned either with Dr. Fordyce's work for the Government or with his daily habits—at what hours he was away from the house working with Professor Fosdick at the university laboratory, how much time he spent in his own private laboratory in the converted garage, whether what he did there had any connection with the project in which he was engaged with Fosdick, and so on. Did the boy happen to mention any of these things to you?"

"No," I answered. "From what he said, I gathered that Miss Hilton's questions were principally concerned with the reason for his father's opposition to his going into a theatrical career. But Mark will be here shortly, and can tell you more about them himself."

"That's what I'm counting on," he replied. "But in the meantime, I'm hoping you may be able to help me get a line on this man, Barto. I understand from Lieutenant McDermott that you were associated with him at the university."

"Not actually associated with him," I corrected. "He was in the dramatics department, while my field is psychology. We ran into each other occasionally at places like the Faculty Club; but other than that, our contacts were practically negligible."

He offered no comment. "I'll not ask you whether there was anything about him to suggest that he might have been an agent for a foreign Government," he said next. "If there had been, he'd never have been selected for the job. But did he ever say anything, possibly during some general discussion at your Faculty Club, which might indicate that he had radical leanings politically?"

I smiled at that. "Quite the contrary," I replied. "Politically, Professor Barto was a staunch Republican."

Mark returned just then, and Harbeson asked him the questions he had first asked me concerning Nora Hilton's interest in his father. Mark's answer must have been a disappointment to him.

"No," he said, "she never asked me anything about Dad's work. In fact, I doubt if she even knew what it was."

The man from Washington asked him a few more questions that bore equally fruitless results; then he brought the interview to a close.

As he was leaving with McDermott, I ventured a question of my own.

"Is it your belief, then," I asked, "that a spy ring was responsible for Dr. Fordyce's murder?"

"It isn't my job to decide how Dr. Fordyce was murdered, Professor Laing," he told me. "That part's up to Lieutenant McDermott. I've been sent here simply to find out whether or not such a ring exists."

I felt that I had been politely but firmly put in my place.

CHAPTER XV

The evening newspapers, in addition to an account of the inquest, carried two stories in connection with the case. The first of these was a humorously melodramatic account of how Deirdre and I—and the policeman, whose name turned out to be Aloysius P. Murphy—had surprised Professor Fosdick the night before rifling Dr. Fordyce's desk in search of some chemistry notes. Evidently Officer Murphy, when he he had talked to the reporters, had decided to write himself into the act from the beginning. He had also embroidered a trifle on details for, as I believe they say in show business, the sake of the laughs.

"That's the trouble with us Irish," Deirdre observed after she had read the account aloud to me: "Our funny-bones are usually located in our heads instead of in our elbows, and sometimes they get to pressing on our brains. Professor Fosdick will be furious when he reads this."

"He'll probably threaten to sue the paper," I commented. "But he'll cool down after a while. What's the other story about?"

The second story wasn't in the least humorous. It concerned Nora Hilton, to whom it now referred as the Mystery Woman in the case. The first part of it was largely a rehash of what had been in the morning papers, again accompanied by her picture and with a few added sidelights on her stage career, evidently gleaned from the obliging Miss Hazel Phipps. But then the paper went on to ask, taking care how it phrased its inquiries so as not to lay its publishers open to possible charges of libel, why, if the police had no one under suspicion of the murder at the present time, they should consider it necessary to find this woman in order that she might either substantiate or disprove the alibi of one of the principals in the case; and if they had such a suspect, why an arrest had not been made. There seemed to be, it pointed out, an abundance of significant clues, and it held up as an example the hat marked with the initials, M. A. F. It next went on, again taking care to make no deliberate inference of any connection between the incident and what it had already set down, to give a detailed account of Dr. Fosdick's interruption of the play rehearsal only a few hours before his death, which the writer of the article must have picked up from someone on campus who had been in the audience that night.

"That tears it, I'm afraid," I said when Deirdre had finished reading. "That story does just about everything but accuse Mark openly of his father's murder. If Nora Hilton isn't found within the next day or so, the district attorney's office is almost certain to step into the case;

and when it does, Mark will be arrested and bound over for the grand jury whether McDermott likes it or not. I was hoping it wouldn't have to go that far."

"Isn't there anything you can do to prevent it, Paddy?" Deirdre asked anxiously.

"No," I answered, and made no effort to keep the discouragement I felt out of my voice. "There's nothing anyone can do until that woman is found—or unless a new lead presents itself; and there's little likelihood of that."

However, a new lead did present itself that very same evening, though when it was first offered to me, I failed to recognize it for what it really was. It came in the form of a telephone call from Prentiss.

"Could you come over to my house for an hour or so, Laing?" he asked. There was in his voice the familiar hush-hush quality, pompously proper yet at the same time pleasurably shocked, which I had come to recognize from past experiences as an almost never-failing indication that the thing he wanted to discuss with me was some more or less scandalous indiscretion on the part of certain members of the student body. "I have—er— run across something within the past few hours which I believe I should at least talk over with you."

"Is it a school matter, Dr. Prentiss?" I inquired, wishing that the classes in Freudian psychology had never been included in my curriculum.

"Indirectly, I suppose it could be considered a school matter, since certain members of the university person-

nel are involved in it," he replied cautiously. "I'd prefer
not to say more than that over the telephone."

I told him I would be over at once, and we both rang
off.

"It must be something pretty serious this time for him
to be taking that attitude," Deirdre observed when I
had told her where I was obliged to go and why. "And
to ask you to come out this evening when it looks as
if it were going to rain," she added with a woman's
solicitude regarding such matters. "Don't let him draw
you into anything if you can help it, Paddy. You've got
enough to worry you just now."

I promised her I wouldn't, and set out.

The feeling of the impending rain which Deirdre had
mentioned was heavy in the air as I left my own house,
and the first big drops of it had begun to fall by the
time I reached the dean's on the other side of the
campus. His housekeeper—Prentiss is a bachelor, and
lives alone—admitted me and showed me into the living
room, where he was waiting.

"I deeply appreciate your consenting to come over
this evening, Laing," he began with nervous effusive-
ness, which made me more certain than ever that something of a more than ordinarily scurrilous nature was
in the offing, "particularly in view of the state of the
weather, and since I realize that you have been—er—
more than ordinarily occupied during the past few
days."

I refrained from pointing out to him that to a college

professor, a request from his dean is tantamount to a command from any other man, come hell or high water.

"It occurred to me that you wouldn't have sent for me unless the matter was urgent, Dr. Prentiss," I replied instead, and hoped he would gather from that that I wasn't anxious to be burdened with it unless it was absolutely necessary. Also, that he would see fit to get down to business immediately, and let me go home.

But he didn't. He fussed about for a full five minutes, adjusting a window shade, switching on (or off) a table lamp, offering me cigarettes, and when I explained that I'd prefer my pipe if he had no objections, insisting upon lighting it for me; a service which, although well meant, I always abhor. It was evident that, now that I was there, he was having difficulty in getting to the subject which had prompted him to send for me.

When he could think of no other excuse for delaying matters, he at last took the plunge.

"As to the matter which inspired me to call you, Laing," he began, standing in front of the empty fireplace, "I must confess I find it a little perplexing to decide upon the proper starting point. But perhaps I had best begin with our—er—visit to Professor Barto's apartment yesterday afternoon, and work both backwards and forwards from there at the same time."

It sounded like a neat trick if he could do it, I reflected privately. Then the full import of what he had just said forced itself into my consciousness, and I literally jerked to attention. Instead of the sort of thing I had expected to hear, he was about to tell me something which might possibly prove to have a bearing upon the murder of Dr. Eric Fordyce!

"You may remember," he went on, and I could tell from his slight change of tone that he had observed my quickened interest and was secretly gratified by it, "that while we were there, I discovered a framed photograph of Helena Stedman upon his desk. You will also remember, I have no doubt, the—er—conversation regarding her which a small group of us indulged in at the Faculty Club a few weeks ago."

I nodded without speaking, while my momentarily aroused curiosity began to wane. Apparently, after all, this interview was to resolve itself into nothing more vital than Prentiss's reminiscences upon a dear, dead lady who had once been the object of his youthful infatuation.

"Finding the photograph there on Barto's desk," he continued, "recalled that conversation to my mind; and this afternoon, finding myself with a free hour or so at my disposal, I went over to the library and got out the newspaper files of twenty years ago to refresh my memory on certain details of the—er—incident we were discussing.

"But before I tell you what I found there, I had best digress for a moment to explain something which is necessary to your understanding of it," he interrupted himself. "Although Professor Barto is listed in our university catalogue simply as Antonio Barto, his full name is actually Marco Antonio Ferrera y Barto. You are familiar, I take it, with the Spanish custom of combining the surnames of both a child's father and mother in the child's own surname?"

I replied that I was, and prayed silently that he'd soon get to the point—if there was a point. What connection there could possibly be between Barto's full name and the actress, Helena Stedman, was so far a complete mystery to me.

"However, he informed us when he came here that since obtaining the American citizenship several years ago," Prentiss resumed, "he has used only the shorter form of his name as being more in keeping with his new nationality, and that he preferred to be known by it alone. But bear in mind that his right name is Ferrera y Barto."

Again he paused, while I writhed inwardly.

"I think I have now provided sufficient explanation for you to grasp the significance of the thing I found in the newspaper files." He got down to it at last. "The name of Helena Stedman's lover and the father of her child was Marco Ferrera."

CHAPTER XVI

"Great Lord!" I exclaimed as I finally grasped the significance of the thing toward which he had been so circuitously leading. "Then he and Barto could be the same man!"

"They *are* the same man," Prentiss stated. "There were pictures of Ferrera in several of the papers, and while they portrayed a much younger and handsomer man, the resemblance was unmistakable. Professor Barto *is* Marco Ferrera."

I remained silent while I turned this astonishing revelation over in my mind. No wonder Barto had left so abruptly that evening at the Faculty Club when Prentiss had been telling us the story of Helena Stedman and her romantic misadventure, and even less wonder that he had given vent to his emotions in that impassioned outburst against the public that had condemned her afterwards! I remembered how I had wondered at the time whether the intensity of his feelings upon the subject might not have arisen from some application of it to his own life in the past. How close to and at the same time how far short of the actual truth my speculations had fallen!

But so far as I coud discover, there was nothing about the fact that the man we knew as Antonio Barto had been the actor, Marco Ferrera, who, as the illicit lover of the once famous Helena Stedman, had been one of the principals in a sensational Hollywood scandal that had furnished hot copy for the newspapers some twenty years ago, to link it with the murder of a quiet-mannered scientist who had in all probability never been anywhere near Hollywood in his life. Neither, for that matter, could I discover any reason why Prentiss should have summoned me to his house to tell me about it.

Then of a sudden I thought I had the answer: He was afraid that some newspaper reporter with a long memory might make the same discovery he had, and blazon it over his front page. That sort of publicity, involving one of its professors in an amour which must have been the talk of its day, would be an even greater catastrophe so far as the university was concerned than the murder had been. He had probably sent for me to ask if I could think of any way that an occurrence of such a highly embarrassing nature could be avoided.

"So far as I know," I began, thinking to put his mind at ease temporarily at least, "Barto's name hasn't been associated with the murder—at least in the newspapers. Until it is, you have nothing to worry about."

He appeared not to have heard me. It was evident that, now he had become launched on his theme, nothing was going to turn him aside until he was finished with it.

"That evening at the Faculty Club," he went on, assuming something of his classroom manner when about to deliver a lecture on Chaucer, "I was not given an opportunity to complete my story. I will do so now."

He crossed to a chair facing the one I occupied, and sat down. "I had ended, I believe," he continued then, "at the point where Helena Stedman had received her divorce from her husband one month after the birth of her child—and Ferrera's. At the time, no provision was made in the divorce settlement for the custody of the child, since there was no question of its paternity. Ferrera, as I recall, even had the unbelievably bad taste to boast about it to the newspapers."

"It seems to me that any such arrangement was hardly necessary under the circumstances," I observed dryly.

"So it would seem, on the face of it," he replied with a slight clearing of his throat. "But there is a certain point of law with which you are probably unfamiliar. It provides that if a married woman gives birth to a child by a man other than her husband, that child is nevertheless regarded as the husband's in the eyes of the law, and he is responsible for it to the same extent as he would be if it were his by blood."

"The devil you say!" I exclaimed, becoming interested in spite of myself. "Are you going to tell me next that Helena Stedman had the effrontery to demand that her husband be made to contribute to the support of another man's child, particularly after her marriage to him had been dissolved?"

"No, no," Prentiss denied quickly, "nothing like that. But along with the husband's legal responsibility for the child, seeing that he and Helena Stedman were still married at the time of its birth, went certain legal rights. He could lay claim to it the same as though it were his own. And that is precisely what he did do."

"Great Lord!" I cried, aghast. "What a Machiavellian way to take revenge upon his wife for her unfaithfulness! He must have loved her very deeply to have come to hate her so intensely."

"The courts did not look at it in the light of revenge," Prentiss replied. "They listened to his charges that Helena Stedman was an unfit mother for the child because of her flaunted immorality, and in the end he was awarded its custody.

"It's said that Miss Stedman fainted when the decision was handed down, and had to be carried from the courtroom. Later she attempted to have it set aside by appealing the case to a higher court, and for over a year the litigation was continued, accompanied by a blow-by-blow description in the public press. But in the end the ruling again went against her. After this second defeat, she gave up and gradually dropped from public sight. Her theatrical career had, of course, already been ruined by the adverse publicity and the public opinion which it aroused. A year or so later, she died in Mexico City."

He paused, and it was impossible to tell whether it was in tribute to the dead actress or because he had reached the end of his story.

"What was Ferrera's attitude in the matter of the custody suit?" I inquired. I found that I was not yet quite able to identify the actor, Marco Ferrera, in my own mind with Professor Antonio Barto.

"According to all accounts, he was beside himself with rage," Prentiss replied, "although it was never entirely clear whether his fury was occasioned by the loss of the child or humiliation in the knowledge that he had been bested in the matter—but perhaps it was an admixture of both. On one occasion during the second custody suit, he and the husband chanced to come face to face on the steps of the courthouse. It was reported that Ferrera rushed at the other man with a knife, and would probably have killed him if onlookers had not interfered. At any rate, he threatened, within the hearing of at least a hundred people, to kill him either then or at some future time. The episode resulted in his being arrested and given a short jail sentence, so that Helena Stedman was obliged to see the end of her case through alone.

"After the suit was finally settled, the husband took the child and went abroad with it, either because he was afraid that Ferrera might attempt to make good his threat when he was released from prison, or simply because he, too, wished to drop from public sight. How long he remained abroad, I have no idea."

He stopped speaking, and this time it was evident that he had come to the end of his account.

I dragged my mind back to the present, aware that he was waiting for me to voice some sort of comment.

"I can appreciate your being anxious to avoid having a scandal of that sort raked up in connection with a member of the university personnel, Dr. Prentiss," I said then. "But as I remarked before, Professor Barto's name hasn't even been associated with the murder of Dr. Fordyce. And unless it is—"

He interrupted me. "But now there is no longer any question that it won't be," he declared, "and the ironical part of it is that I, the dean of the College of Arts and Sciences, shall have to be the one to make the association. Don't you understand, Laing? That was the primary purpose behind my sending for you this evening. Now that I have inadvertently stumbled upon these particular occurrences in Professor Barto's past, it becomes my painful but unavoidable duty to pass them along to the proper authorities: or, since you are so intimately associated with Lieutenant McDermott, to ask you to pass them along as my representative."

"But why?" I asked, endeavoring to suppress my annoyance. "What you've just told me involves Barto in no crime; or at least in none that is punishable by law."

"Involves him in no crime!" he fairly exploded. "Great heavens, man! Exactly how much evidence do you need to involve a man in the crime of murder?"

"Murder!" As I echoed the word, I had never felt so completely stupid or so completely at sea in my life. "Just how does it involve him in murder?"

"I should think that would be self-evident," Prentiss replied sententiously, and his impatience with what he abviously considered my dullness was apparent in his voice. "Since it can easily be proved that Antonio Barto and Marco Ferrera are the same man, and since he not only had a motive, but made a public threat to—"

He stopped abruptly. "Oh, great heavens!" he exclaimed. "I sincerely beg your pardon, Laing. No wonder you were unable to perceive the connection! In my absorption with the other details of my account, I completely neglected to mention the very point that was most necessary to your comprehension of its significance."

Once more he paused, while I sat waiting and wondering what under high heaven would be coming next.

"When we were discussing the—er—tragedy of Helena Stedman that evening at the Faculty Club," he began afresh, characteristically approaching his objective with a kind of verbal flanking movement, "I believe I remarked that I was unable to recall the name of her husband. Since then, however, I have refreshed my memory from the newspaper files which I examined this afternoon. His name was Dr. Eric Fordyce."

CHAPTER XVII

If Prentiss's first revelation concerning Barto had astonished me, this second one regarding Eric Fordyce left me literally thunderstruck.

"Dr. Fordyce—Helena Stedman's ex-husband!" I gasped as soon as I had recovered myself sufficiently for coherent speech. "Great Lord above! Then Mark Fordyce must be . . ."

"The illegitimate son of Marco Ferrera," he finished for me.

Suddenly the whole thing was blatantly obvious, and I was amazed that I had not suspected it from the moment he had revealed to me Barto's real identity. There was a whole host of significant circumstances which should have sprung to my mind at once. There was Mark's given name, for example—Mark Anthony, Anglicized from the Spanish Marco Antonio. There was Dr. Fordyce's seemingly fanatical opposition to the boy's having any association with the theater—only too understandable and natural now. And there had been his peculiar attitude toward Mark; at once passionately de-

voted and almost cruelly austere. What must have been
the bizarre situation between those two for over twenty
years—the man torn between the love he could not deny
the boy because of his mother and the hatred he could
not banish because of his father, the boy himself loving
his supposed father in return, but unable to understand
his strange treatment of him!

I became aware that Prentiss was speaking again, and
dragged my attention back to what he was saying.

"What freakish circumstance brought those two men
together again at this particular time and place, we shall
probably never know," he declared, and I realized that
he was speaking of Eric Fordyce and Marco Ferrera,
"but the tragic result of their having so met is all too
obvious. Ferrera had sworn to kill Fordyce almost
twenty years ago. He made good that threat just two
nights ago."

He paused, waiting for me to speak, but I remained
silent.

"Don't you agree with me?" he demanded impatiently at last.

"What you say is logical," I admitted slowly, "but it
isn't conclusive. We have no real evidence that Ferrera-
Barto killed Dr. Fordyce, but only his threat to do it
made nearly a quarter of a century ago. And many a
man has threatened to kill another without ever putting
his avowed intention into execution."

"I should think the fact that he has run away—"

Prentiss began, but I cut him short.

"Give me until tomorrow to think all this over before I say anything to Lieutenant McDermott," I requested. Then I resorted to the one argument which I knew would be sure to carry weight with him. "There's no point in laying the university open to the backwash of a double scandal involving a member of its faculty— the old scandal concerning Helena Stedman and the present one of murder—if there's the remotest chance that he may be innocent."

"You think there actually may be such a chance?" he asked hopefully.

"I don't know," I answered. "That's why I must have time to think."

"Very well, Laing, do as you think best," he replied, and I thought I detected a note of relief in his voice at even this temporary respite. "I will abide by your decision, no matter what it may be."

I promised him that I would let him know what that decision was before I acted upon it; then I left.

As I walked homeward through the cool May night, I was completely unaware of the soft rain that was still falling. I now had sufficient evidence to direct suspicion of the murder away from Mark Fordyce and toward Antonio Barto, but at what a price it would have to be to the boy if I decided to use it!

Mark was nowhere in evidence when I reached the house, for which I was grateful, since it afforded me an opportunity to repeat to Deirdre what I had just learned from Prentiss. She was as incredulous as I had been over the revelation.

"Poor Mark!" she exclaimed, characteristically thinking first of the effect that it would be bound to have upon him. "Will he have to be told, Paddy?"

"I don't know how it can be avoided," I replied. "If Barto is guilty, the whole story will have to come out."

"It will be like losing his father all over again," she said. She came over and sat on the arm of my chair. "Do you think there's the remotest chance that Professor Barto might not be guilty after all?" she asked anxiously.

I had been searching for some piece of evidence, no matter how fragmentary, that would sustain such a possibility as I walked back from Prentiss's house, but did not discover any. "I'm afraid there isn't," I admitted. "He had both motive and opportunity. Then there's the evidence of that hat bearing the initials, M. A. F., which we know now could have stood for Marco Antonio Ferrera, that was found in the wreckage of the laboratory. Besides, as Prentiss pointed out, there's the fact that he's run away, which in itself amounts practically to a confession of guilt."

"I know the wicked are supposed to flee when no man pursueth," Deirdre remarked, "but they usually wait until they've a reason for believing that somebody *doth* pursue before they do it. And if Professor Barto kept his

head long enough to have made all those elaborate arrangements for destroying the evidence of his crime by
fire . . ."

She let the sentence trail away unfinished, and for the
next minute or so we both remained silent. At length
she spoke again.

"There's one thing, Paddy, that doesn't seem quite to
fit," she began slowly. "Professor Barto must have
known who Dr. Fordyce was for several months—
probably since he first came here last fall. If he was
going to kill him, it seems more logical that he'd have
done it at once, instead of waiting all this time. It looks
to me as though he'd been planning another kind of
revenge: to take Mark away from Dr. Fordyce by encouraging him to go on the stage, just as the doctor
took him away from Helena Stedman nearly twenty
years ago. And if that was his intention, why should he
have ruined it all, just when he appeared to have accom-
plished his purpose, by creating a serious break between
the two of them, by resorting to murder?"

I had thought of that very argument myself during
my walk home through the rain, but there had been
another factor which counterbalanced it: Barto had
been furiously angry over Fordyce's spectacular interruption of the play rehearsal that night. In addition to
that, the doctor had succeeded in getting the boy to go
home with him. It could have been that, either carried
away by the violence of his rage or believing his original

plan to alienate Mark and his foster father had failed—
perhaps a combination of both—he had resorted to the
surer way of murder.

I explained this to Deirdre.

"I suppose you're right," she acknowledged hope-
lessly. "Besides, there doesn't seem to be anyone else who
could have done it. But at least we won't have to say
anything to Mark—about Dr. Fordyce's not having
been his real father, I mean—until after Professor Barto
has been found."

I agreed with her on that, although I felt that at best,
it would only be putting off the evil hour. Moreover, I
was fully aware that when the time did come, I was the
one who would have to do the telling.

The following day was Sunday. Mark declined Deirdre's and my invitation to accompany us to church,
although he insisted that we go; and so, suspecting that
he preferred to be alone for a little while, we went
without him.

Just before we left, I had a telephone call from
McDermott.

"Harbeson's gone back to Washington," he informed
me. "He said he's going to check the F. B. I. files for
anybody answering to the description of either Barto
or the Hilton woman, and that he'll get in touch with
me if he finds anything; but he didn't sound too hopeful of results. I'm afraid he doesn't think too highly of
our enemy agent theory, Pat, and I've got to admit that

after talking it over with him, I'm beginning to lose faith in it myself. We found out from Professor Fosdick, the man Fordyce was working with on the experiment, that practically all the important data concerning it was kept locked in a safe in his office at the university; yet no attempt was made to get at it. It looks as though, if we're going to continue with the supposition that Barto was in any way involved in Fordyce's death, we'll have to find another motive for him."

"And so far there hasn't been any trace of either Barto or Miss Hilton?" I asked, anxious to steer the conversation away from the subject of motive.

"Oh, we've had plenty of leads on both of them," he replied. "One from as far away as California. But none of them have amounted to anything. If either Barto or the woman had actually been in one half the places they've been reported as having been seen in, they'd have had to be traveling by rocket plane; and even then, I doubt if they could have made it. But I haven't given up hope yet of finding them; the search for them's only been on a little over twenty-four hours."

After promising as usual to let me know the instant there were any developments, he rang off.

As Deirdre and I were returning from church an hour or so later, we ran into Professor Fosdick. He was in a highly indignant and excited state of mind about something, and at first I suspected it must be because of the story of his midnight escapade that had appeared in the newspapers the evening before. But a few minutes' talk with him—or rather, listening to him talk—showed me I had been wrong.

"It's outrageous!" he exclaimed as soon as he had stopped sputtering sufficiently to become coherent. "No wonder this country doesn't advance more rapidly in matters of scientific research for national defense! When it regards its own scientists as objects of suspicion and permits every young upstart of a Junior G-Man with a tin badge pinned under his coat lapel to insult us with impudent questions and gross innuendoes, how can it expect us to put forth our best efforts in its behalf?"

I suggested that the Government, having been once bitten in the matter of the atom bomb secret, had probably become twice shy.

"Stuff and nonsense!" he snorted. "If the Government felt that it couldn't trust me, it shouldn't have given me this assignment in the first place. And what gave this fellow, Harbeson, the idea that poor Fordyce's death might have had anything to do with the work we were engaged in to begin with?"

Like a coward, I shifted the entire blame for that onto McDermott's shoulders, since he was the one who was least likely to have any further dealings with the peppery little professor. "It was merely a possibility that had to be taken into consideration," I explained. "When Lieutenant McDermott, who's in charge of the murder investigation, learned of the work Dr. Fordyce had been engaged in, it became a part of his job to make sure that angle was thoroughly investigated along with every other conceivable lead he could find."

"He has other leads, then?" Fosdick demanded with newly aroused interest.

"None that seem to be getting him any further than this one has," I replied evasively, and made my escape with Deirdre.

CHAPTER XVIII

It was around the middle of the afternoon when the next development in the case came, although strictly speaking I suppose it was not actually a development, but only a complication of affairs already existing. I was alone in the living room listening to the symphony concert on the radio when there came a ring at the doorbell. Knowing that Deirdre was busy in the kitchen with preliminary preparations for dinner, I went to answer it.

A little to my surprise, I found McDermott on the porch.

"I've got to talk to you, Pat," he said as soon as I had opened the door. His voice sounded tired and a little grim. "Can you spare me a few minutes?"

"Of course," I answered, and led the way to my study, where he dropped wearily into a chair.

"What's happened?" I demanded, positive from his manner that something had. "Has there been news of Barto or Nora Hilton?" I had a horrible premonition he was going to tell me that one of them had been found murdered.

But he set my mind at rest on that score, at least.

"No," he answered, "nothing like that. I only wish to God that there were! But there's been a development of another sort.

"The district attorney read that story in last night's paper practically demanding Mark Fordyce's arrest, and this morning only a few minutes after I'd talked to you, he called me up and asked me to come over to his house. He claimed it was for a conference on the case, although as it turned out, the real purpose of it was to take me over the coals for not having held the boy on suspicion pending further investigation, at least.

"Although I didn't consider it any of his business, since technically I'm not under his jurisdiction nor accountable to him in any way for how I see fit to conduct an investigation, I told him I hadn't felt it would be advisable to do anything about Mark until the Hilton woman had been found and we'd got her story. If she substantiated his alibi, we'd only have to turn him loose again and look pretty damned foolish in the bargain; and besides, I was investigating this other angle that seemed to involve her and Barto directly in the murder. He asked me what that was, but when I'd told him, he wasn't impressed. In fact, he went out of his way to point out to me that the only thing I had to link either of them with the murder was my own imagination. In the end, he gave me forty-eight hours to locate Nora Hilton and get her story."

"And if you don't . . ?" I asked as he paused.

"If I don't," he answered, "he's going to act without

me and swear out a warrant for Mark's arrest, charging him with the murder of his father."

I felt as though an icy hand had suddenly fastened itself about my heart. The thing which I had been dreading for the past two days was apparently upon me.

"Pat, we've got to think of something!" McDermott exclaimed in a kind of fierce desperation. "Something that'll stall the D. A. off until the Hilton woman can be located. If we don't . . ." He didn't bother to finish the sentence.

"We've still got those forty-eight hours," I reminded him feebly.

He gave a short, bitter laugh. "What are forty-eight hours when we don't even know where to look for her?" he demanded. "That sort of thing takes time, and plenty of it. Oh, a miracle could happen, I suppose, but it's not the kind of thing we dare count on. A good, plausible motive for Barto is what we need now."

"You're convinced, then, that Barto's your man?" I inquired.

"It's got to be either Barto or Mark," he replied, "and by this time, I'm as convinced of the boy's innocence as you are. On the other hand, we know that Barto was engaged in slimy business of some kind, and that the Fordyces were the object of it. On top of that, he's run out. Anybody but a pig-headed district attorney could see that that adds up to something. If only we could discover what the connection was between Barto and Fordyce, or why he should have hated the doctor enough to want to kill him. Haven't you any ideas, Pat?"

I had. I could have told him what Prentiss had told me the evening before, and directed him to those twenty-year-old newspaper files, where he could have read all he needed to know. But I remained silent.

It wasn't reluctance at the thought of throwing one man to the wolves in order to save another that kept me so, for by that time, I was fully convinced of Antonio Barto's guilt. It was because of Mark. If I told McDermott what he wanted to know, the whole ugly story would have to come out, to be smeared for a second time all over the front sheets of the public press. How would the boy take the shame and humiliation of learning that, instead of being the son of Dr. Eric Fordyce, he was only the illegitimate offspring of the man who had murdered Fordyce? On top of everything else he had been through, it might prove too much for him to bear, and he might break under the added burden. Had I the right to thrust such knowledge upon him, when for twenty years Dr. Fordyce himself had contrived to keep it from him?

On the other hand, had I the right to remain silent when doing so was almost certain to result in the boy's arrest? Or when it might be tantamount to shielding a murderer?

I became conscious that McDermott was speaking again; had, apparently, been doing so for several seconds without my being aware of it.

". . . And you know the district attorney," he was saying. "Once he gets his hooks into somebody, he won't bother to look in any other direction, no matter what else might turn up. Oh, I know I could continue to work on the case alone up to the very minute when the jury brought in its verdict—and after that, if necessary. But I'd have to do it entirely on my own, and a case of this kind isn't a one-man job. Unless we can dig up some way of making the D. A. see that Barto's just as much of a suspect as Mark is, I'm afraid we're sunk."

"What about the report Harbeson promised to send you from Washington on the foreign agent angle?" I asked, at my wits' end. "Couldn't you at least get him to hold off until that gets here?"

"It wouldn't help," he answered. "Harbeson promised he'd get that report to me by Tuesday morning, and the forty-eight hours won't be up until then."

I said nothing for a moment or two; then I asked, "Mac, can you give me until this evening to think this over? By that time, I may be able to come up with something."

"I hope to high heaven you do," he declared fervently, "for the Lord knows, my brain's practically burned out a bearing trying to think of a way out."

When he had gone, I reflected with a grim smile that my principal occupation lately seemed to be asking people for time to think; Prentiss the evening before, and now McDermott. I returned to my study, and sat down wearily at my desk to wrestle with the problem of how to save young Mark Fordyce from arrest without at the same time revealing to him the secret of his parentage.

But after an hour of mental wrangling, I found that I had arrived absolutely nowhere. Still those two incontrovertible facts stood out alone, as they had done at the beginning: If I told the thing which would supply Antonio Barto with a motive for the murder, young Mark would be branded for the rest of his life with the shame and disgrace of it. If I did not tell it, he would be arrested, possibly even convicted, for a crime he had not committed. There seemed to be no middle course.

I tried to tell myself that even if Mark were cleared of suspicion at the eleventh hour by some miraculous intervention on the part of Providence, the case would not end there. McDermott would go on with it until he had collected sufficient evidence to fasten the guilt upon Barto, and then the truth would come out in any eventuality. What matter, therefore, if it came out now or later? But even in the face of this argument, I could not bring myself to act.

At last, driven to extremity, I fell back upon the weak philosophy of procrastination: There remained almost forty-eight hours before the district attorney would take action. I would wait until they had expired; then, if an unfeeling Providence still refused to intervene in the boy's behalf, I would reveal what I knew.

Only half satisfied with what I realized was merely a begging of the question rather than a solution to it, I decided to go for a brief walk before dinner. If the fresh air and slight exercise did not aid my mental processes, they might at least help me to throw off the feeling of depression that had settled upon me.

As I opened the front door to go out, a woman's voice spoke only a foot or so in front of me, and I realized that I had surprised a visitor about to ring the doorbell.

"Are you Professor Laing?' she inquired. There was a tense quality about her voice which suggested that she was in some sort of emotional state which she was endeavoring to keep under control.

I affirmed that I was.

"There's something I've got to tell you, Professor," she hurried on. "May I come in?"

Although I had never heard her voice before in my life, I knew without being told who it was that spoke to me.

"Of course," I answered, stepping aside and holding the door open for her. "Please come in, Miss Hilton."

CHAPTER XIX

She had seated herself in the living room before it apparently dawned upon her that I had called her by her name.

"How did you know who I was?" she demanded then, and there were both suspicion and a vague uneasiness in her voice. "You couldnt have recognized me from that picture in the papers. Hazel told me you were blind."

"It was your unusual perfume," I explained. "I passed you once before when you were wearing it, and one of the people with me told me who you were."

"Oh, so that's it!" She sounded relieved. "I thought for a minute maybe you were psychic or something, and it kind of scared me. Not that I believe in such things exactly, but—well, you never can tell."

She dismissed the subject abruptly, and got down to the matter that had brought her. "I suppose you know why I've come here?" she suggested.

"Because of Mark Fordyce?" I inquired.

She must have nodded, for she didn't reply at once verbally; then, realizing that I was unable to see the gesture, "You've guessed it," she affirmed: "it's because of Mark. The papers said he needed me to back up his story about last Thursday night."

"That's so," I replied. "And you've no idea how relieved I am that you've come, Miss Hilton, nor how relieved Lieutenant McDermott will be when he learns of it. Incidentally, do you mind if I send for him, so that he may hear what you've got to say, too?"

But she raised an objection to that.

"Hold it!" she exclaimed. A harsher tone had come into her speech, breaking through the veneer of culture that had been there in the beginning. "I'm not telling this to any cop. Not that I'm afraid to talk in front of one," she added quickly, as though fearful that I might come to some erroneous conclusion. "It's just that I want you to hear what I've got to say first by yourself. You'll understand why when I've said it."

Wondering a little, I assured her that it should be as she wished.

This seemed to satisfy her, although I could tell that even then, she did not completely relax.

"After I left the kid last Thursday night," she began abruptly, "I decided to drive back to New York, and write Hazel Phipps to send my clothes up after me. As for Tony Barto's car, I thought I'd leave it at a garage somewhere along the road and go the rest of the way by train, then get Hazel to tell Tony where he could pick it up if he wanted it. I knew he'd be fit to be tied when he found I'd run out on him, and I didn't want him coming to New York after me and maybe beating my brains out with that hot Spanish temper of his. Anyway, I left the car at a place in Newark, saying I wanted the motor overhauled, and that I'd be back for it in a day or so."

"Yes, I know," I told her. "Lieutenant McDermott traced it there."

"I thought some smart cop would do that, once they found I'd taken it," she remarked parenthetically. "But at the time, I'd no reason to suspect the cops would be looking for it—or me either."

She dismissed the matter of the car as though it were of no further interest, and returned to her original theme:

"Then last night I read in the paper about the murder, and how Mark needed me to prove his alibi. The story didn't come right out and say so, but it made it pretty clear that if I didn't show up, he'd be under suspicion of having killed his old man. Well, I hadn't done anything I needed to hide from the police about, so I decided to come back and do what I could for the kid."

She paused, and I heard her fumbling with something, presumably her handbag. "Mind if I smoke?" she asked. "I can talk better when I've got a cigarette to sort of steady me."

"Please do," I replied, and rose to hold my lighter for her. As her hand touched mine while she guided the flame of the lighter to the tip of the cigarette, I noticed that her fingers were icy cold. Was it fear of Antonio Barto, I wondered, that had made them so? She had spoken of being afraid he might follow her to New York and kill her, although that might have been only a figure of speech.

"I got here around noon today," she resumed after she had taken a puff on the cigarette, "and went straight to my old room. Hazel was there, and she told me about how you'd been around a couple of days ago asking for me. That gave me an idea. I knew who you were from having heard Mark talk about you, so I decided that instead of going to the police with my story right away, I'd come to you first. You see, I wasn't sure whether a part of what I had to tell had anything to do with why Doc Fordyce was murdered and who murdered him or not, and I didn't want any nosy cops finding out about it in case it didn't."

Again she paused, evidently for another puff on the cigarette; then she continued:

"Professor Laing, what Mark told you and the police was the truth. We did go off together to be married that night, and he was with me in Barto's car until nearly one o'clock. I'll admit I wasn't in love with him, and I know he wasn't in love with me. He was feeling sorry for himself and a little scared because of the way he'd walked out on his old man, and he wanted somebody he could sort of hang on to. For my part, I'd got the bright idea that if I actually married the kid, maybe I could get Doc Fordyce to pay me a nice hunk of cash to get me to agree to an annulment.

"Then as we were driving along and my brain began to get its second wind, I realized that if we played it the way Tony Barto had planned, the doc wouldn't be in the picture to buy me off. That made me think twice about going through with the marriage. What would be the point of it if I wasn't going to get anything out of it?

"But that wasn't the only reason I decided to back down." A note of deeper earnestness came into her voice. "Maybe you'll think I'm making this part up, Professor Laing, just to make it sound good for myself, but I swear to you it's the truth; if it wasn't, I'd never have told you the other part to begin with. I couldn't have gone through with that marriage even if there had been a chance of a shake-down afterwards, because it would have been too rotten a trick to play on a nice kid like Mark Fordyce.

"Maybe I'm not a real lady," she gave a short, self-mocking laugh, "but I've played the part of one often enough on the stage to know the right kind of words to say so I'll sound like one, and to cross my feet at the ankles instead of my legs at the knees. I guess I must have picked up a couple of other things, too, one of them being that you don't take advantage of people who trust you. Anyway, before I fully realized what I was doing, I'd brought the car to a stop and told Mark he'd better just forget about me and go home to papa, or words to that effect.

"I could tell right away that by that time, he didn't want to go through with the wedding business any more than I did, although at first he pretended to protest like a little gentleman that he is. So to help him save his face, I deliberately picked a fight with him. It ended with him getting out of the car and marching off down the road, just like he told you, while I drove on toward New York."

I became conscious of a respect for Nora Hilton that I had never expected to feel. A real lady she might not be, as she herself had admitted; but in this instance, at least, she had displayed attributes that would have been a credit to the best of them.

She had stopped speaking and sat as though waiting for any questions I might wish to ask. I had one ready for her.

"You said a moment ago, Miss Hilton," I began, "that if you played it the way Barto had planned, Dr. Fordyce wouldn't be in the picture to pay you off. What did you mean by that?"

I heard the spurt of a match as she lighted a second cigarette.

"That's part of what I wanted to tell you before I went to the police," she said then. "You see, Tony Barto brought me here in the first place to deliberately play up to Mark and help turn him against his old man by making him believe the doc was being unfair to him in forbidding him to go on the stage. He said a woman could accomplish that sort of thing better than another man could, but I knew that what he really meant was that he wanted me to—"

She broke off abruptly. "Say, are we alone here?" she demanded. "Or is there somebody else around?"

"My wife is in the kitchen," I replied. "Mark, who's staying with us for the present, went out a little over an hour ago. There's no one else in the house."

"I guess I'm a little jumpy today." She gave a nervous laugh. "I thought for a minute— But to get on with what I was saying:

"Tony promised he'd pay all my expenses and buy me clothes and whatever else I needed to do a good job, and he kept his word. I was to have five hundred dollars besides if I could get Mark to run out on his old man and go back to New York with me. Well, like I said just now, I've played the part of a lady often enough on stage to be able to play one off of it when I wanted to; and besides, I wasn't exactly behind the door when they passed out the looks. Anyway, Mark fell for the whole set-up right from the beginning. He'd never known a real actress before, and I guess he thought I was something extra special. I let him go on thinking so, because I wanted that five hundred dollars.

"Then all of a sudden last Thursday night as we were driving along toward the state line, the sliminess of the whole thing hit me. I decided I could get along without Tony's five hundred dollars if I had to earn it by probably lousing up that nice kid's whole life. That's why I made up my mind to go back to New York and forget about the whole thing.

"I knew Tony would be red-hot mad when he found out what I'd done, because when I first came here, he'd told me why he was engineering the whole scheme to break up Mark and Dr. Fordyce. And that's why I came to see you first, Professor Laing, instead of going straight to the police—because I've got a notion that what he told me may have something to do with Dr. Fordyce's murder. But first," she hesitated, and I sensed that she was glancing over both shoulders to make sure there was no one around who might overhear, "you've got to promise me you won't repeat it to the police or make me tell it to them myself unless you feel absolutely certain—"

She broke off the sentence in the middle, and I heard the legs of her chair scrape against the floor as she sprang up from it.

"What's the matter, Miss Hilton?" I exclaimed, rising also, for the woman's action had told me that something had happened to alarm her.

Her answer came in a frightened, breathless gasp: "Theres a man outside on the porch! He's coming in here! He looks as if—"

Her words died away as the latch of the screen doors giving onto the side porch clicked, and someone stepped into the room.

I swung about to face the intruder. "Who are you?" I demanded. "And what do you want?"

He didn't answer, but I could hear the rasping sound

of his heavy breathing as he stood there just inside the room.

"Who are you?" I repeated, taking a step toward him. "Answer me, or—"

Nora Hilton's terrified scream cut across my words: "Professor Laing, he's got a gun! He's going to—"

The last part of her sentence was drowned in the roar of the revolver.

CHAPTER XX

I wasn't near enough to the woman to catch her as she fell, and I heard her body strike the floor with a limp, sickening thud. The next instant running footsteps were racing across the living room.

I made a leap in their direction, and for an instant felt the rough fabric of a man's coat beneath my fingers, but it was jerked away before I could grasp hold of it. Momentarily thrown off balance, I stumbled to my knees. Before I could get to my feet again, the front door slammed.

I made my way to where a faint moan told me Nora Hilton had fallen, and knelt beside her. As I put out my hand to touch her, I felt something warm and sticky on the front of her blouse.

Dairdre came running in from the kitchen. "Paddy, what's happened?" she demanded. There was fear for my own safety in her voice. "Are you—" She stopped as she must have caught sight of the figure on the floor, beside which I was kneeling. "Oh!" she gasped, and now the fear in her voice was blended with horror. "Who is she, Paddy? Is she . . . ?"

"She's Nora Hilton," I replied. "Someone came in from the porch and shot her while she was here talking to me. I don't know yet how badly she's been hurt."

Fortunately Derry has never been one of the type that faints at the sight of blood. She helped me get Nora Hilton's unconscious form onto the sofa, then bent over her to examine her wound.

"She's been shot in the chest, just over the heart," she reported almost at once. "It looks bad, Paddy. Phone for a doctor while I get some towels to staunch the bleeding."

But I had taken hold of one of the woman's wrists just in time to feel the faint thread of pulse flutter out beneath my fingers.

"I'm afraid it's too late for that, Derry," I said. "Nora Hilton is dead."

I released the limp wrist with a feeling of grim irony. Nora Hilton had been murdered to prevent her from telling me something which I already knew.

There came a heavy step on the side porch, and the same screen doors through which the murderer had entered were thrust open again.

"What's been goin' on over here?" the voice of the policeman who had been on duty at the Fordyce house two night before demanded. "I thought I heard a revolver shot, and it sounded like it came from— Holy Mother of God!" He broke off as he caught sight of the woman's body on the sofa. "Who's she and who shot her?"

"She's Nora Hilton, the woman we've all been trying to find," I replied, and explained what had happened. "You'd better report this at once to Lieutenant McDermott," I finished. "The telephone's over there on the writing desk; or if you prefer, you can use the extension in my study across the hall."

"Nora Hilton—and her dead!" he muttered as he crossed to the nearer phone. "The lieutenant's goin' to jump out of his skin when he hears this."

I thought that would probably be only a slight exaggeration.

It took McDermott less than fifteen minutes to get out to the house. He was accompanied by several plainclothes men and followed only a few minutes later by the county coroner.

"This is one hell of a bad break, Pat," he said. "We find the Hilton woman—or she turns up voluntarily— only to lose her again, this time for good. Did she have a chance to tell you anything before she was shot?"

"Yes," I answered. "She corroborated Mark's alibi in every detail. She also explained the relationship between herself and Barto."

Then while two of the plainclothes men tested the screen doors through which the murderer had entered for fingerprints, and two others examined the side porch and the ground bordering it for possible footprints, I repeated to him the conversation which had taken place between Nora Hilton and myself.

"So she was killed to keep her from telling why

Barto wanted to break up Mark and his father," he observed when I had reached the end of my account. "That makes it pretty plain that his motive for it must have been the same motive that led him to kill the doctor. But what under God's blue heaven could it have been! Why should Barto have been interested in breaking up the relationship between a father and son, and then have murdered one of them on top of it? What did he have to gain by it?"

I realized that the time had come when I could no longer remain silent without being guilty of deliberately obstructing justice, and reluctantly I opened my mouth to tell him what that motive had been. But before I could speak, he forestalled me with a question.

"When the murderer ran past you, Pat," he asked, "and you caught hold of his coat sleeve for a minute, was there anything to tell you that he was Barto?"

"No," I was forced to admit. "My hand merely brushed his arm at the shoulder as he dodged out of my grasp. All I could tell was that he was a man of approximately my own height wearing a coat of some medium-weight worsted material; which could mean that he was Barto or any one of a hundred other men."

"That's the devil of it!" he exclaimed in disgust. "We know he's our man, but we can't prove it. If only she'd mentioned him by name before he shot her!"

"I'm just as happy that she didn't," I remarked dryly. "For if she had, I probably wouldn't be here to tell you about it."

"I suppose you're right about that," he admitted. He called to the policeman who had run over from the Fordyce house after the shot had been fired.

"You, Murphy," he demanded, "where were you while all this was going on? The commissioners going to raise holy Moses when he finds out a murder was committed here in broad daylight and with a cop not more than fifty feet away."

"I've only got one pair of eyes in me head, Lieutenant," Murphy replied, offended, "and I was usin' them to watch the house next door. Nobody said a word about watchin' this house."

"All right, all right." McDermott waved the explanation aside. "But now try using them and your ears too to find out whether anybody in the neighborhood noticed a man either skulking around or running away from this house at about the time the shot was fired. When you've finished, come back here to me and report."

The policeman hurried off on his errand, obviously glad of the excuse to get away.

Just then the coroner, who had been examining Nora Hilton's body at the other end of the room, came up and joined us.

"You'll probably want to know what I found before I leave, Mac," he said to the lieutenant, "although I don't know what good it's going to do you in helping you catch your murderer. Anyway, here it is: The bullet entered between the fourth and fifth ribs, punc-

turing the lobe of the left lung and severing the large
artery leading from the heart. Death resulted primarily
from internal hemorrhage."

"Got any idea of the size of the gun that shot her,
Doc?" McDermott inquired.

"It's a little difficult to tell from the size of the entrance wound alone," the coroner replied, "but I'd say
off-hand that it was probably a thirty-eight. We can't
be sure, though, until I've removed the bullet, when
your ballistics men can decide."

He left then, promising to send his men around to
remove the body as soon as the police photographer had
finished with it.

After the coroner had gone, McDermott called to
one of the two plainclothes men who were going over
the frame and latches of the screen doors for fingerprints. "Having any luck, Donaldson?" he inquired.

"I'm afraid not, Lieutenant," the plainclothes man
answered. "The guy who did the shooting must have
wrapped his handkerchief around the handle of the
latch, for we've brought out what looks like the weave
of a piece of cloth. There was a big fat thumbprint
right in the middle of it, and for a minute I thought we
had something there, but it turned out to be Murphy's,
left when he ran over here and pushed the door open
after he'd heard the shot."

McDermott swore. "Is that all you got?' he demanded.

"All except for two sets of prints—a man's and a

woman's—on the framework of the door, both of them
repeated a couple of times and overlapping," the detective replied. "And they probably belong to Professor
Laing and his wife. But we've still got the inside of the
doors to do," he added on a more hopeful note.

"And you can put in your eye what you're likely to
find there," McDermott grunted in disgust. "I don't
know why the department bothers to train men for
fingerprint work any more," he complained to me. "No
criminal with an ounce of brains leaves prints now-a-
days, while the other kind leave plenty of other clues
lying around for us to trace them by." He turned back
to the plainclothes man. "When you're through there,
go back to headquarters and find out whether a permit
to carry a gun was ever issued to Antonio Barto," he
directed. "If one was, notice whether the gun was a
thirty-eight calibre."

"I can start now if you want me to," the man said.
"Mitchner, here, can finish this job."

McDermott told him to go ahead; then, since the
police photographer was beginning to set up his camera
to photograph the body, we went into my study across
the hall to be out of the way.

"I got a report yesterday from the man who's back-
tracking on Barto," McDermott remarked then. "He's
found that before coming here, Barto taught in a dramatic school in New York for a couple of years, while
before that he worked as both an actor and a director on
Broadway. He's got no criminal record, and so far as

my man's been able to discover, there's never been any connection between him and Fordyce, at least, during the New York period. So it's beginning to look as though either we'll have to go back further than that to find the connection—if there was one—or else start looking for the motive in something that occurred after both of them became associated with the university."

I wondered what he would say when I told him that the motive for the murder had originated out of something which had occurred nearly twenty years ago, and for the second time within less than an hour I steeled myself to make the revelation.

"Mac," I began, "there's something—" But before I could go any further, Fate again intervened. There was the sound of footsteps crossing the hall, and the police photographer came to the door of the study.

"I've taken four shots of the body and two long shots of the room, one looking into it from the doors to the side porch and the other looking toward them, Lieutenant," he reported. "Are there any other pictures you want me to take before the coroner's men get here?"

"Not that I can think of," McDermott answered. "But wait a minute, and I'll go back there with you and take a look around just to make sure."

He returned to the living room with the photographer, and for the second time the moment that had been ripe for telling him about the connection between Antonio Barto and Eric Fordyce passed.

There were no other pictures that he wanted taken,

so he told the photographer he might leave. While the man was packing up his camera and tripod, the policeman, Murphy, returned from his canvass of the neighborhood in search of anyone who might have seen the murderer either approaching or leaving the house.

"Only one person admits havin' seen anything, Lieutenant," Murphy announced when McDermott had asked him the result of his errand. "That was an old maid in the house directly across the street—Miss Sarah Heisy, she said her name was—with a tongue on her you could use to peel potatoes."

"Never mind her tongue," McDermott cut in impatiently. "What did she see?"

But the policeman wasn't to be hurried. "When I first asked her my question," he went on, "she acted like she thought lookin' out of her own front windows was one o' the deadly sins, and I'd insulted her by even suggestin' that she might have done it. But finally she got around to admittin' that she'd happened—just *happened*, mind you—to be at her livin' room window fixin' something at the curtains when the shot was fired, and that a minute later she saw a man come runnin' outa the front door of this house and head up the street. She said he was wearin' a light grey suit and a grey felt hat about two or three shades darker than the suit, that he was pullin' it down over his eyes as he ran, so that she couldn't see his face, but that she got the feelin' there was something familiar about him, as if she'd seen him around here before. That was all she could tell me—except what she thought of the police force for lettin' murders be committed right on people's doorsteps."

McDermott turned to me. "Did Barto ever come here to see you, Pat, that he should have seemed familiar to her?" he asked.

"No," I answered. "But I've heard it said that Miss Heisy has X-ray eyes, and knows all the comings and goings from here to the far side of the campus. He could have seemed familiar to her because she'd noticed him somewhere else."

"If she's that kind, probably every man for miles around would have looked familiar to her," he commented. "Well, I suppose the best we can hope for is that once we've caught him, she may be able to pick him out from a half-dozen or so men all wearing light grey suits and darker grey felt hats."

Just then the plainclothes man, Mitchner, who was still at work on the screen doors, called to him from across the room.

"I've just turned up a third set of prints, Lieutenant," he said. "They look as if they'd been made by a rather small man. But they're in sort of a funny position to have been left by the murderer if he came in through these doors and left by the front door."

"What d'you mean, Mitch?" McDermott asked as he and I crossed over to where the detective was standing. "Oh, I see!" he exclaimed the next minute, then added for my benefit, "The thumb is below the other fingers instead of above, as it would have had to be if he'd reached back to push the door shut behind him as he came in. These prints were made by a man who was facing the door, about to go out."

"They're probably Mark's," I offered. "He went out through those doors about an hour before Miss Hilton got here."

"I imagine you're right," McDermott agreed absently. "Anyway, we can check with him to make sure." Then, as though the fact of the boy's absence had just penetrated his consciousness, he asked, "Incidentally, where is Mark? I thought he was staying here with you?"

Before I could answer, there came the sound of the front door opening, and a second or two later Mark himself entered from the hall. He stopped short at sight of McDermott, the plainclothes man, and the policeman.

"What's happened?" he asked in quick apprehension. "Has there been an accident of some kind?"

The policeman, Murphy, whose ready Irish wit seemed to have taken a somewhat grisly turn, answered him before either McDermott or I could think of an adequate reply.

"Plenty's happened, sonny," he pronounced. "But it was no accident. The murderer did it on purpose."

CHAPTER XXI

"Murderer!" Mark echoed the word as though it had left him momentarily stunned. "Who . . ?"

I took a step forward with the intention of placing myself between him and the dead body of the woman on the davenport; but I must have misjudged my distance, and he saw past me.

"Nora!" he cried, and while there was both shock and horror in his voice, he made no attempt to approach her. "How did she get here? What—what's happened to her?"

I explained in a few brief sentences without filling in any of the details.

"Then it was on my account that she was killed!" he exclaimed. He sounded as though the thought made him feel a little sick. "If she hadn't come back to help me, she'd never have been killed! It's almost as if, in a sense, I were to blame."

I tried to tell him that this was not so, but I doubt that he even heard me. The thought that he had been the indirect cause of Nora Hilton's death seemed to have taken possession of him to the exclusion of all else.

"By the way, Mark," McDermott put in, "where were you about an hour ago?"

He had to repeat the question before Mark became aware of it. Then the boy swung upon him in a kind of desperate defiance.

"So you're starting that again!" he choked. "You think I actually did kill her because of that quarrel we had after she'd backed down about marrying me last Thursday night, just as you thought . . ." He was unable to finish the sentence.

"No, son," McDermott said, and there was genuine kindliness in his voice. "Quarrel or no quarrel, I'm not such a fool as to think you'd kill her when you knew she was your only chance of proving your alibi on the other count. I'm merely trying to clear you from the beginning for the sake of the record. Now suppose you tell me what I want to know."

"I was taking a walk with Lee—Miss Lee Laurence," Mark answered, still a little sullenly. "She's a student here at the university, and lives at the women's dormitory. We walked through the botany gardens behind the chemistry and biology buildings for a little while; then we sat down on one of the benches to talk. We were there until maybe about fifteen minutes ago, when I took her back to her dormitory and then came straight here. Does that satisfy you?"

"It does," McDermott replied tersely, and offered no further comment, although I knew that later he would have to check the story with Lee as a matter of form.

I thought the boy would protest when the plain-clothes man, Mitchner, asked his permission to make a record of his fingerprints, but he didn't. Either he accepted McDermott's explanation of the purpose for which they were wanted, or he had concluded that it would do him no good to raise an objection. After the prints had been taken and Mark had affixed his signature to the card on which they were recorded, McDermott and his men left.

As they were leaving, the men from the coroner's office arrived to remove the body of Nora Hilton. Mark watched them take it away in stony silence; then he turned, still without a word to anyone, and went upstairs to his room.

Deirdre, who had withdrawn from the scene shortly after McDermott's arrival, now rejoined me in the living room.

"This room will never seem the same again, Paddy," she declared with a little shudder. "Every time I come into it, I'll see that poor girl lying there on the sofa."

"We'll get a new sofa," I promised her, "and you can have the room redecorated if you like. I'll even help you change the furniture about."

She didn't respond to my clumsy attempt at lightness. "I feel terribly sorry for Nora Hilton," she said. "She came back here of her own free will to help Mark, not because he meant anything to her, but simply because it was the decent thing to do; and she was killed for doing it. Somehow it seems more dreadful that way than it would if she had really been in love with him."

"Try not to think about it, Derry," I advised her, and wished secretly that I could stop thinking about it myself.

Mark didn't come down to dinner that evening, and I didn't blame him. Deirdre and I felt little like eating ourselves: the tragedy of only a few hours earlier was still too close to us. Around eight o'clock, however, the boy came down to my study, where we had gone in preference to the living room.

"If it isn't asking too much, Professor Laing," he began diffidently, "could I talk to you about what's happened?"

"Of course, Mark, come in," I replied at once; while Deirdre, sensing that he might feel less restraint if he were left alone with me, made some excuse about having things to attend to in another part of the house, and withdrew.

But even after she had gone, he seemed vaguely embarrassed, as though he were having difficulty in deciding just how to open the subject he wanted to discuss with me. To help put him at his ease, I pushed my tobacco humidor across the desk toward him and invited him to join me in a pipe, knowing that like most of the Senior boys at the university, he had taken up pipe smoking as a kind of symbol of masculine maturity.

We smoked in silence for a minute or two; then he said abruptly:

"Professor Laing, it's about Nora that I wanted to

talk to you. She told me once that she had no living relatives, so there'll be nobody to make arrangements for her funeral. Do you suppose people would misunderstand if I were to take care of everything?"

By "people," I knew he meant primarily Lee Laurence.

"No, Mark," I answered, keeping up the polite fiction that we were talking about the public in general, "I don't think anyone would misunderstand. In fact, they'd probably think more of you for doing it."

He seemed relieved by that. "It's not that I was ever actually in love with her," he explained carefully, as though he wanted to be certain that I receive no wrong impression on that point. "I've known that definitely ever since last Thursday night. But I was fond of her in a different sort of way, and I believe that in her own fashion, she rather liked me, too. Besides, it was on my account that she was killed." He paused a moment, then asked, "Have they any idea who it was that shot her?"

"Both Lieutenant McDermott and I believe Professor Barto may have been involved," I admitted.

"Professor Barto!" He was incredulously amazed by that. "But I thought she was killed by the same person who killed Dad. I mean—" he fumbled for the right words to express what he wanted to say, "Professor Barto didn't even know Dad. Why, I doubt if he ever so much as set eyes on him before that time at the Little Theater building last Thursday. What motive could he have had for wanting to kill him?"

It was an excellent opening for me to tell him the whole story, but I refused to take advantage of it. Instead, although I stuck to the literal truth in my reply, I told him only a part of it.

"We can't be too sure that Professor Barto and your father didn't know each other, or at least have some contact, in the past," I said. "On the contrary, we're beginning to have reason to suspect that they did. You see, Mark, Nora Hilton wasn't killed because she'd come here to corroborate your alibi; she'd already done that before she was shot, although the murderer must have been standing out there on the porch listening all the while she was talking, and could have stopped her at any time he chose. It was because she was about to tell me something else—something which she'd implied concerned you and your father."

"Something that concerned Dad and me?" he repeated, genuinely puzzled. "What could Professor Barto possibly know about us that would make him commit murder?"

The simple logic of the question struck me with unexpected force. Why *should* Barto have been willing to commit murder to keep it from becoming known that he, and not Eric Fordyce, had been Mark's father? To conceal the fact that he had had a motive for the murder of the doctor? But if he had run away in the first place because he believed he would fall under suspicion, it could have made little difference to him whether his motive were known or not; at least, not sufficient dif-

ference for him to have risked recognition and capture
by returning to the neighborhood of his first crime in
order to silence Nora Hilton. Besides, he must have
realized that the former connection between himself
and Eric Fordyce would be brought out in any case as
soon as the police had dug back far enough into their
pasts.

I tried to recall the woman's last words to me just
before she had been shot. "When I first came here, he'd
told me why he was engineering the whole business to
break up Mark and Dr. Fordyce," she had said. "That's
why I came to see you first instead of going straight to
the police, because I've got a notion that what he told
me may have something to do with Dr. Fordyce's murder." There was nothing in that, surely, to hint at anything other than what I already knew, or that McDermott wouldn't find out eventually through the ordinary
police channels.

There had followed a little more about my first
promising not to repeat what she was about to tell me;
then she had been interrupted by the appearance of the
murderer at the screen doors, and had cried out—

Of a sudden the significance of those last few seconds
struck me: It was not what she had said, but what she
had *not* said that was important! And almost on top of
it came the realization of other things; things which I,
like everyone else connected with the case, had taken for
granted because there had been no apparent reason for
questioning them. But now they were taking on an en-

tirely new meaning in regard to the case as a whole. It was like hearing a musical theme, which had hitherto been played only in a minor key, suddenly transposed into a major. It left me feeling a little dazed, for I knew now that I held in my hands the solution to the whole mystery.

But now another problem confronted me: Although I had my solution and was convinced in my own mind that it was the correct one, I had no proof of it. And without proof, there could be no case, and consequently no conviction.

In a way, I was glad that this was so; for knowing what I now did, I felt only pity for the man. How could I be sure, I asked myself, that in his place and with his provocation, I too might not have been driven to kill? Besides, there was Mark to be considered. Twenty years ago, a woman and two men had sown the wind. Now it was he who would have to reap the whirlwind.

But at least he would no longer be under suspicion of murder. Nora Hilton's statement to me just before she had been killed had cleared him of that; and even though now she would never be able to repeat it to the proper authorities, I knew that my own repetition of it had carried sufficient weight with McDermott.

An idea whereby I might obtain the evidence necessary for the conviction of the real killer flitted across my mind, but I put it from me. After all, I was not officially connected with the police; it was not up to me to collect evidence. It would be enough if I told McDermott of my suspicions—for in the eyes of the law, they were no more than that—and left the rest to him. Or for that matter, I need tell him nothing. A man's opinion is one of the few things he is still permitted to keep to himself.

But even as I told myself these things, I knew that my arguments were futile. No man, regardless of the circumstances, has the right to condone murder, either by actual deed or by merely holding his peace. Besides, there had been the killing of Nora Hilton, for which there were no extenuating circumstances.

I hadn't realized how absorbed I had been in my own thoughts until Mark spoke.

"What's the matter, Professor Laing?" he asked curiously. "You look as though—" he gave a brief laugh— "somebody had just burst a paper bag in your face."

"And that about describes the way I feel," I admitted. "Something *has* just burst in my face, and it's left me a little stunned." I paused a moment, making a final mental survey of the thing I had in mind; then I said, "Mark, I'm going to have to do something that I can't explain to you. I wish I didn't have to do it, but I must. Will you trust me, and try not to think, either now or later, that I've been your enemy instead of your friend?"

"I could never think that of you," he replied with boyish warmth. Then he asked, "Is there anything I can do to help with whatever it is you've got in mind?"

"Yes," I answered. "Go over to the women's dormitory and ask Lee to take another walk with you. I've got to send for Lieutenant McDermott, and I don't want you to be here when he arrives."

I waited until he had gone; then I picked up the telephone and called McDermott. It was the most difficult thing I had ever done in my life, for it was the first step in a plan to use Mark Fordyce as bait for a trap which, if it worked, would lead to the conviction of his own father for murder.

CHAPTER XXII

McDermott came promptly in response to my guarded hint over the telephone that I had an urgent matter to discuss with him.

"Now what's it all about, Pat?" he demanded when he had settled himself in the same chair which Mark had occupied only a little while before. "Have you thought of a way that we can link Barto to the murders, or how we can find him?"

"I already know where Barto is," I answered. Then, before he could ask me where, "But before we can link him to the murders, there's something I want you to do for me, Mac: I want you to arrest Mark Fordyce, charging him with both killings."

"You *what!*" he fairly yelped. "Are you out of your mind? I thought you were the one who was so positive of his innocence."

"I still am," I replied. "But it's got to appear to the general public for a little while that the police believe him guilty if we're to catch the real murderer."

"I'm beginning to see," he said slowly. "You believe that once he hears that somebody else has been definitely charged with the murders, he'll consider himself safe and come out of hiding, is that it?"

"I believe he'll do something like that," I replied evasively.

McDermott remained silent for almost a minute; then:

"I won't deny it would get me off of a pretty bad spot to do what you suggest," he admitted. "The D. A. called me up around dinner time this evening to ask me whether we'd turned up anything yet on Nora Hilton; I think he was beginning to regret even those forty-eight hours he'd given me to find her in. He hadn't heard about what happened here this afternoon, and when I told him, he acted as if he held me morally responsible for it. You see, according to his reasoning, Mark's now guilty of both murders."

"You mean he refuses to believe that Nora Hilton was telling the truth about his alibi?" I asked.

"Either that, or that you were when you repeated her story to me," he replied candidly. "He didn't make himself too clear on that point. But on this point he did make himself clear: What Nora said to you in private can't be regarded as evidence now that she's dead, since it would be only hearsay testimony. What's more, he doesn't believe Miss Laurence's corroboration of Mark's alibi for the second murder. He says that since she's obviously in love with the boy, she'd lie to shield him.

"All of which adds up to the very reason why I can't

jump at the chance to save my own neck by placing his in jeopardy," he summarized. "For suppose Barto didn't rise to your bait. On the one hand, we couldn't arrest Mark, then turn him loose again after a few days for no apparent reason; the D. A. would never agree to that. And on the other, we can't let him stand trial for crimes we're both morally certain he didn't commit. How would we be able to get him out of the mess once we'd get him into it?"

I didn't answer his question directly. "And if you don't arest him now, then what?" I inquired.

He made no reply to that, so I made one for him. "The district attorney will probably do it himself in any event," I pointed out. "He'll make certain first that there's enough evidence against the boy to warrant his asking for an indictment; then he's even liable to demand that the commissioner remove you from the case so that he can act with a free hand. And now that Nora Hilton's dead, there will be no argument you can use to stop him."

I paused a moment; then I added, "Mac, I've got a theory of this case that I'd like to put to the test, but I can't do it unless Mark is definitely taken into custody. The law permits you to hold him for twenty-four hours without entering a formal charge against him. Do that, and if at the end of that time I haven't provided you with an irrefutable solution to both murders that will satisfy everybody from the district attorney on down—or up . . ."

I didn't finish the sentence. There was no way I could have finished it.

"Yes, I can hold the boy that long without actually booking him," he admitted, still only half decided. "And it can be implied to the newspapers that he's been definitely charged. But are you sure this theory of yours will work?"

"It's got to work," I replied grimly.

He agreed then, but he asked one more question. "Mark understands that this will be only a fake arrest, doesn't he?" he inquired.

I had to confess that I had said nothing at all to Mark about my plan.

"But, good Lord, man!" McDermott exclaimed, outraged. "You've got to tell him! You can't let him believe—"

"Please, Mac," I interrupted, "let me play it my way. We can't take chances of endangering the whole scheme by letting anybody know the truth, not even Mark."

What I could not tell him was that it was bad enough to have to use the boy as I was about to do without making him a conscious party to it. Even the painful alternative of obliging him to believe for over twenty-four hours that he had actually been placed under arrest was preferable to having him find out later that he had assisted knowingly in a plan which was to result in the apprehension of his own father.

"Very well," McDermott agreed unwillingly, and his tone implied what he thought of the whole arrangement. "But I still feel that you're putting the lad to an unnecessary mental hardship, Pat. He'll be held incommunicado for the entire time; he couldn't give the show away in any case."

I made no answer.

Mark was taken into custody when he returned to the house a little after eleven o'clock that night. At first he was too stunned even to protest his innocence, but just before he left with McDermott, he turned to me.

"You still believe in me, don't you, Professor Laing?" he asked, and there was pleading in his young voice. "You know I never killed my dad?"

"Yes, Mark, I do," I assured him. For a moment I almost relented from my purpose and told him the truth. But I knew that if I did, he'd have to live with the knowledge afterwards; and so I forced myself to remain silent.

"A little while ago, I asked you to trust me," I reminded him instead. "Try to remember that for the next twenty-four hours. At the end of that time, I shall be in a position to establish your innocence beyond any possibility of doubt. I promise it."

After he and McDermott had gone away together, Deirdre came over and stood in front of me. "Why did you promise him that, Paddy?" she asked. "You know that if you were able to establish his innocence within the next twenty-four hours, you could have talked Lieutenant McDermott into waiting that long."

"Yes," I admitted, "but I didn't want to talk him into it, Derry."

She rested her hands upon my shoulders, and I could tell that she was studying my expression.

"So having Mark arrested is part of a plan to prove he isn't guilty," she guessed shrewdly. "But why couldn't you have told him that?"

Then, partly because I knew it was useless to try to keep a secret from Derry, and partly because I had to talk to somebody about it, I told her the whole truth.

When I had finished, she buried her head against my coat and cried a little. "It's all too horrible," she whispered. "If only there were some other way!"

"But there isn't, Derry," I told her. "I've got to go through with it as it stands."

"I know," she answered. "There's nothing else you can do."

The following morning the newspapers were full of the story of Mark's arrest. McDermott had handled that end of it well in his dealings with the reporters. He had furnished no details, but had told them merely that the police felt there was now sufficient evidence to warrant the boy's being held in connection with both murders. What that evidence was, he promised, they would be told when the proper time came. The impression created was that the prosecution intended to reserve its case until Mark should be arraigned before the grand jury.

Fortunately, Lee Laurence didn't learn what had

happened until the close of classes that day. When she did, she descended upon Deirdre and me like a young hurricane.

"It's outrageous!" she stormed, beating her fists against the arm of the chair into which she had thrown herself upon her arrival. "Anybody in his right mind would know Mark would never have killed his own father—or the Hilton woman, either," she added as an afterthought. "It just goes to show how stupid the police really are." She turned to me. "Pat, can't you do something about it?"

"He's already doing everything that can be done," Deirdre said in my defense. Then she added a touch of her own that I never would have thought of. "But don't you understand, Lee? Mark is really better off in jail for the present. After the way the papers have been practically accusing him of his father's murder and demanding his arrest, some crank might have decided to take matters into his own hands, and . . ." She left the rest of it to Lee's imagination.

It had the calculated effect. "I hadn't thought of that," Lee admitted soberly; then to me again, "But he won't have to stand trial, will he, Pat? You won't let it go that far?"

"I won't if I can help it," I assured her, and prayed with silent fervor that I might be able to.

Around six o'clock that evening, I received a telephone call from McDermott.

"So far there's been no sign of Barto," he reported,

"although I've had half a dozen picked men on the look-out for him at bus and railroad terminals and a half-dozen more around the university, as well as the entire city police force alerted. If he doesn't show within the next five hours, I'll be forced either to release Mark or book him on the murder charge. Which do you want me to do?"

I hesitated. "Don't give up hope until you have to, Mac," I counseled him finally. "Anything can happen within those five hours." Then I asked, "Where are you speaking from?"

"I'm in my office at police headquarters," he answered. "In fact, I've been here since nine o'clock this morning, just on the chance that Barto might show himself and be picked up."

"Stay there for the remainder of the evening," I directed. "If by a quarter to eleven neither of us has had any luck, we can decide then what's to be done."

Although I could tell he wasn't satisfied, he agreed to do as I asked, and rang off.

While I had no definite reason for believing that the break in the case would come within the next few hours or that it would come to me rather than to Mc-Dermott, I nevertheless had an almost uncanny conviction that it would be so. Accordingly around seven o'clock, I spoke to Deirdre with as much casualness as I could muster.

"Lee is probably in her room at the dormitory worry-ing about Mark," I observed as we sat together on the porch. "Why don't you call her, Derry, and ask her to go to a movie with you? It might take her mind off her troubles for a little while, at least."

"I was about to call her and ask her to come over here," Deirdre said.

"I think the movie would be better," I persisted.

But I should have realized I would be no more successful in keeping a secret from Derry this time than I had been the evening before.

"Paddy, why are you trying to get me away from the house?" she demanded; then in quick suspicion, "Are you expecting *him* to come here?"

I didn't attempt to deny it. "But he won't come unless he's sure I'm alone," I added, "for he knows his safety depends on that."

"But you'll be putting yourself in danger," she protested. "He's already killed twice. How can you be sure he won't . . ?"

"I'll be in no danger," I assured her. "If he comes at all, it won't be for the purpose of killing."

"I still don't like it," she persisted. "Suppose he suspects it's a trap?"

"In that case, he'll stay away," I replied. "Besides, it isn't a trap in the ordinary sense of the word. He'll be free to leave any time he wants to."

She gave in then, although I could tell that she considered it against her better judgment, and went into the study to call Lee on the telephone extension.

"I wish you'd have Lieutenant McDermott or some

other police officer hidden in the house, just in case anything goes wrong," she said when she had returned to the porch where I waited for her. "I'd feel a lot safer in my mind for you if you did."

"No," I answered, "I want him to be free to act wholly upon his own initiative. He's entitled to that much, regardless of what he may have done."

"I suppose you're right," she admitted reluctantly, and set out to meet Lee.

As I listened to the sound of Derry's light footsteps retreating into the quiet evening, I reflected how, although Helena Stedman had been dead these many years, she had remained even after death a ruling influence in the lives of three men—her former husband, her lover, and her son. Now I was about to put that influence to the test, to prove whether or not it was strong enough to bring one of them to the aid of another, even though the cost to himself would be the highest a man can be asked to pay.

I waited until the sound of my wife's footsteps had ceased to be even an echo against the surrounding stillness; then I went into the living room, where I switched on all the lights and opened the slats in the Venetian blinds, so that anyone watching from outside the house could easily see I was there alone. After that, I settled down to wait.

CHAPTER XXIII

The minutes crawled into a quarter, a half, and finally a full hour, and I was still alone in the room. Several times I heard the hollow sound of footsteps approaching along the sidewalk, but they always passed by without stopping or even hesitating. Was my strategy not going to work after all? I asked myself. If it failed, it wouldn't be because of any flaw in my deductive reasoning, of that much I was certain; for I was positive that I had solved the case correctly, even if I was not in a position to prove my solution. The question was whether, in using Mark's apparent arrest to bait my trap, I had overestimated my man.

The silence of the empty house was beginning to grow oppressive. I thought of turning on the radio, but hesitated to do so for fear the sound of the music might drown out any other sound I was waiting to hear.

My pipe, which I had lighted at the beginning, had burned itself out long ago. I was about to refill it when I thought I detected the faintest whisper of a sound, which might have been only the gentle night breeze rustling the foliage outside the house, but which could have been a guarded footfall ascending the steps to the side porch. But since I wasn't at all certain, I went on with what I was doing and pretended that I had heard nothing.

After a moment it came again, and this time there could be no mistaking it: Someone was out there on the porch. Then came a tiny metallic click, which I recognized as the slipping back of the latch on the screen doors.

I gave the man time to ease the door open several inches; then I spoke. "Come in," I invited, and called him by his name.

I heard the sharp hiss of his breath as he released it in a startled gasp. "How did you know?" he demanded, abandoning all further effort at stealth.

"That you were there, or who you were?" I asked.

"Both."

"I heard you when you first stepped up onto the porch," I replied. "As to how I knew your identity, that will take a little longer to explain, and I imagine you have more pressing business."

"I have," he admitted grimly. "But before we get down to that, you'd better close those blinds."

I rose to obey, but before I could pull the cord on the first one, he stopped me.

"Wait," he commanded. "Better leave them as they are."

I understood the reason for his change of mind. "If

you think my closing the blinds was to be a signal to the police that you're here," I said, "you're wrong. Neither the police nor anyone else is watching this house, because no one but myself had the faintest idea that you might be coming here tonight."

"Nevertheless, we'll leave the blinds as they are," he decided. "I'll sit over here, where I can't be seen from the windows."

He crossed the room in two quick strides to where there was a chair whose high winged back would effectively hide him from anyone passing in the street.

"So you deliberately arranged matters so that I could see you were alone in the house," he observed when he had seated himself. "How did you know I was coming?"

"I assumed you'd had time to read in the papers of Mark's arrest," I replied, "and that you'd be anxious to find out if you could just what the evidence is against him, and whether the police will be likely to make their case stick."

"And will they?"

It was impossible to tell whether there was concern in the voice or not, but the question had come just a fraction of a second too quickly to be entirely disinterested.

"I think they will," I answered, weighing my words carefully. "There's the circumstance of the quarrel, which they know about now, and the evidence of the hat bearing his initials, while in the murder which occurred this afternoon—"

"The hat wasn't his," he interrupted me.

"Perhaps not, but only you know that." I paused for the space of a second or so; then I added, "Besides, now that Nora Hilton is dead, there's no one who can substantiate his alibi."

He gave a suppressed exclamation, as though this were something he hadn't realized before.

"You still haven't explained the reason for tonight's preparations," he pointed out after a moment: "why you should have arranged for me to come here without fear of being recognized—sending your wife away for the evening, then turning on all these lights and opening the slats of the blinds so that I could be sure you were alone. Why did you do it, Laing?"

"Because I happen to be convinced of Mark's innocence," I answered. "But I can't prove it without your help."

"What makes you think I can help you prove it?" he asked curiously.

I hesitated the barest instant before replying, because I wasn't too sure how he might take my next disclosure; then I said:

"The fact that I know it was you who committed the two murders of which he stands accused."

He made neither an indignant denial nor any elaborate pretense of incredulity that I should have made such a statement.

"Do you realize," he asked casually, "that if what you

say is true, I might put a bullet through your head from where I'm now sitting at any minute?"

"Yes, I realize that," I admitted, and prayed he wouldn't guess that it was precisely what I had been afraid he might do, "but I don't believe you will. You are not a killer by instinct, therefore it isn't likely that you could commit an unnecessary murder; and you are well aware that it would be unnecessary for you to murder me in order to insure your own safety. The two of us are alone here in the house; there will be no witnesses to anything that may pass between us. If I were to repeat any of it later, there would be only my unsupported word in proof of it. In fact, there would be only my unsupported word that this interview ever took place at all."

"You seem to have thought of everything," he remarked with a slightly cynical note in his voice. "Everything, that is, except why, if I did kill these two people as you claim and have so far succeeded in escaping even the merest breath of suspicion, I should now throw away my safety—maybe even my life—in order to save Mark."

"He is your son," I pointed out.

"He is *not* my son!" he cried in a sudden fierce burst of passion.

I let that pass unchallenged, for I believed he was unaware of the full import of what he had said.

"Moreover," I pursued, "you committed at least one if not both of these murders on Mark's account in the first place. That in itself is an indication of your wish to protect him. Besides, if you weren't concerned about him, why did you come here this evening?"

I heard him make an abrupt movement, as though he were thrusting aside the motives I had attributed to him. "You're wrong," he contradicted. "I killed the first time for revenge, and the second for my own protection. As to why I came here tonight, it was to make sure the case against him was complete, that there was no chance of his being acquitted and the investigation reopened—"

He stopped, suddenly conscious of what he was saying.

"You admit, then, that you are the killer?" I asked quietly.

He gave a short, mirthless laugh. "Since, as you pointed out a few minutes ago, we have no witnesses to what we may say or do here tonight, I can think of no reason why I shouldn't," he retorted with a sudden flare of bravado. "Yes, of course I'm the killer—I like that word, incidentally, much better than murderer. But I'm interested in learning precisely what motive you've ascribed to me for my crimes. Not, I hope, that revolting incident which took place at the theater last Thursday night."

"No," I answered. "A man doesn't commit murder because of a college play. You killed so that Mark might never learn he was the son, not of Eric Fordyce, but of the actor, Marco Ferrera."

He caught his breath with a startled, whistling sound. "So you found that out, too!" he exclaimed. "Tell me how."

"It was the names," I told him. "It was as easy to make Marco Ferrera out of Marco Antonio Ferrera y Barto as it was Antonio Barto. Then, too, the name Eric Fordyce isn't precisely a common one."

"And you remembered after all these years," he muttered. "Yet you must have been only a very young boy at the time."

I didn't tell him it had been Prentiss who had refreshed my memory, for I had no wish to let him know that another beside myself shared at least a part of his secret. After all, he had already killed two people who had known.

He rose abruptly from the chair where he had been sitting, and I heard him take several rapid turns up and down the room.

"Tell me," he jerked out at length, "how did you know it was I who had killed him? Was it the circumstance of the fire?"

"No," I answered. "The significance of that never occurred to me until after I had got my initial clue from quite a different source. It was the murder of Nora Hilton that first put me on the right track."

He halted in front of me. "Of Nora Hilton!" he cried in protest, as though he considered this an unfair trick of Fate. "But that was the one in which I felt absolutely safe from suspicion! How did it tell you anything?"

"Nora didn't know her killer," I explained. "If she had, she would have mentioned his name instead of crying out merely that there had been a man hiding outside on the porch. But she did know Mark, which proves it wasn't he whom she saw, and who shot her. And she also knew Antonio Barto. The only man connected with the case whom she did not know was you, Dr. Fordyce."

CHAPTER XXIV

For a moment after I had spoken, Fordyce said nothing, as though he were turning my explanation over in his mind. At last:

"Neat," he approved. "Very neat indeed!" There was genuine admiration in his voice. "You're to be congratulated, Laing. But can you prove that it was I who shot her?"

"Unfortunately, I can't," I admitted. "For that matter, I can't even prove that you're alive—or that you killed Antonio Barto."

"Then what are you going to do about it?"

I didn't answer for a second or two; then:

"The question isn't what *I* am going to do about it," I said gravely, "but what *you* are going to do."

"I?"

"Yes, you. Are you going to clear that boy in the only way he can be cleared, or are you going to let him be sent to the electric chair?"

He turned away from me. "He won't get the death penalty," he flung back over his shoulder. "He's too young."

"But not young enough for it to weigh against the enormity of his supposed crimes," I pointed out. "The murder of his own father and of the woman who had refused to marry him. Boys younger than twenty have been executed for less than that. There will be little sympathy for him, I'm afraid, in the minds of any judge and jury."

"But if it were shown that he couldn't be guilty of one of the murders," he argued, "it would follow logically that he couldn't be guilty of the other. And you can prove he didn't kill Nora Hilton, even if you can't prove who did."

"Not prove," I corrected him. "Perhaps raise a reasonable doubt in the minds of some of the jury, but that's all. There will be others who will argue that the mere circumstance of Nora Hilton's having failed to call her murderer by name just before he shot her is no sure guarantee that she hadn't recognized him."

"And so," he observed cynically, "you expect me to throw away my life to save the life of Marco Ferrera's son?"

"No," I answered. "To save the life of Helena Stedman's son."

"Helena Stedman ceased to mean anything to me from the day she sullied herself with that common actor," he shot back defiantly. "From then on, my love for her was changed to hate, and I lived for only one thing: to make her suffer as she had made me suffer. That was why I took the child away from her."

" 'Never undertake to interfere in other people's lives, just because an illogical quirk in the law has given you the power to do it,' " I quoted softly; " 'for the satisfaction it promises at the outset soon turns into a burden that is too great for any mortal man to bear.' "

He was silent, recognizing his own words spoken to me that evening when we had walked home together over three weeks before.

"It's true," he acknowledged at last, and his voice was so low I barely caught the words, "it did become a burden. More than that, it became an excruciating torture. At first I tried to hate the boy because of his father. To help me in this, I even continued to call him by Ferrera's Christian name, which had been given to him at his birth, although I shortened it to Mark. It seemed appropriate, for his mother had branded him even before he was born with the mark of—"

He broke off, and for nearly another minute, silence lay between us.

"A little while ago," he said then, "you spoke of him as my son. In a sense, you were right, for without realizing it at first, I gradually came to look upon him in that light—as the son Helena and I might have had if things had been different. I suppose that was why I never told him about his real parentage; I'd let myself believe that his thinking he was my son would in a sense make it so. Ironic, isn't it," he gave a harsh laugh, "that I should have found myself actually fathering the illegitimate offspring of my wife and her lover!

"Then as the boy grew older and his interest in the theater began to manifest itself, the real torture started. For to me it indicated only one thing: his natural father, whose very existence I had denied, was cropping up in him in spite of anything I could do. I determined to suppress it at no matter what cost."

Again he fell silent, but this time for only a few seconds; then he resumed:

"After we returned home from the theater last Thursday night, Mark and I had the first real quarrel of our lives. We were both too infuriated to control ourselves or to realize half of what we were saying, and recriminations were made on both sides which neither of us meant. It ended with Mark's packing a suitcase and rushing out of the house, swearing never to return.

"After he'd gone, I had time to cool off and to begin to regret my part in the affair. I even determined that when Mark came back, I'd apologize for having humiliated him publicly back there at the theater; for it never entered my head that he'd meant what he'd said about not coming back.

"I was still sitting up waiting for him at twelve o'clock when there came a ring at the doorbell. I jumped up and hurried to answer it, thinking it was Mark, who'd probably forgotten his key in his hurry. Instead, it was Antonio Barto—I'll continue to call him that, for at the time I didn't recognize him as the man he really was.

"I judged he'd come to talk to me about letting Mark

go on with the play, and while I wasn't in the least anxious to discuss the subject with him at that time, I invited him inside, where I made some sort of half-hearted apology for my earlier actions and offered to do whatever I could to make amends.

"He waited until I'd finished; then he chuckled to himself as though he were secretly amused by some aspect of the situation that only he was in a position to appreciate, and told me there was no need for me to make amends about anything, since I'd already played perfectly into his hands. I asked him what he meant by that, and he answered that by my own actions that evening, I'd alienated Mark from me for all time, and driven the boy to him. When he saw that I still didn't understand, he grinned at me openly with all the malice of an incarnate devil, and told me who he was."

"Did he say anything more?" I inquired when he had stopped speaking, and it had begun to seem as though he might not go on without prompting.

"He said much more," he replied, and now his voice had become thick with the memory of it. "He told me how Helena had died a little less than two years after her divorce from me, and he accused me of having hastened her death by taking her child away from her. Then he told me how, through all the years that followed, he had kept track of me, how he had watched me being torn between my growing affection for Mark and my hatred of his parentage, and had gloried in my mental torture. He boasted of how he could have stepped in at any time to ruin both our lives by his mere presence, but that he had preferred to wait until Mark had attained young manhood, then to take him away from me in a manner which would prove that the boy was his son spiritually as well as physically, and not mine.

"He admitted that when he learned I was coming here to work with Professor Fosdick on some experimental research for the Government, he had deliberately followed me. The only coincidence involved was that there should have been an opening in the dramatics department of the university just when he needed it, and that he should have succeeded in getting the appointment. After that he had cold-bloodedly set about cultivating Mark's friendship and winning his confidence. He told me how he had even brought a second-rate actress, Nora Hilton, from New York to infatuate the boy and encourage him to go on the stage in open defiance of my objections, and that he had good reason to know Mark was with her at that very moment. He finished by announcing that he intended to climax his revenge by telling the boy who he really was, and the circumstances of his birth.

"When he said that, something inside my head seemed to snap. The seething hatred of the man that had been fermenting in me for over twenty years suddenly burst its bonds, and I seized him by the throat. He struggled like a maniac in my grasp, but his very struggles only lent fuel to my rage.

"At last he went limp in my hands, and I flung him away from me. He landed in a heap where I had thrown him, and lay still. When he didn't get up after a minute or so, I bent over him to drag him to his feet. It was then I discovered I had killed him."

Once more he stopped speaking, and I could hear the harsh rasping of his breath in his throat, as though he were reliving that death struggle. This time, however, he went on again without prompting.

"My first thought was to telephone the police and make a clean breast of everything. Then I realized that if I did that, Mark would find out the very thing I most wanted to keep from him. My best course seemed to be to conceal the body and to say nothing.

"But a dead body isn't an easy thing to conceal, especially when you've only a limited time at your disposal. For all I knew, Mark might return at any minute and discover everything. Then I remembered that little explosion I'd had in the laboratory a few weeks ago, and it gave me the solution to my problem."

"Was that when you decided to pass Barto's body off as your own?" I asked.

"No," he answered, "that didn't occur to me until after I'd carried it out to the laboratory and was saturating it and its surroundings with chemicals to make it burn more quickly. I knew I couldn't hope to destroy it completely in the fire. Fragments of charred bone, at least, were almost certain to be found, which would have to be accounted for. Besides, when it was discovered that Barto had disappeared, somebody might perceive a connection. But if the body could be identified as mine, everything would be neatly taken care of. In fact, it even seemed possible that someone who had seen the murderous rage that had been in Barto's face that night when I had dragged Mark away from the theater might put forward the theory that it was he who had killed me. You see, by that time my first reckless feeling that it mattered little what became of me had passed, and the natural instinct to preserve my own life had begun to assert itself.

"I took from my finger the ring which I always wore, and slipped it onto his. Then I placed in one of his pockets a watch that had my name engraved inside the case. After that I struck a match, tossed it into a pile of waste paper that I had prepared, and left the building.

"When I got back to the house, I discovered Barto's hat lying on the chair where he'd left it, so I made a second trip out to the laboratory with it. The fire was well under way by that time, so I simply tossed it in through the door without noticing where it fell. It must have been an old hat he'd had for a long time, for I noticed the initials, M. A. F., for Marco Antonio Ferrera, stamped on the sweatband. It never occurred to me that it might not be destroyed in the fire, but found later and mistaken for one of Mark's because of those initials.

"My next move was to go downtown and rent a room

under an assumed name at a small hotel. I felt perfectly safe in doing this, for I am a very ordinary-looking man who can pass through a crowd without attracting a second glance from anybody. Moreover, since it would be assumed within another few hours that I was dead, no one would be looking for me, and there would be no occasion for second glances in any case. I've been there ever since, except for yesterday afternoon when I came back here and shot Nora Hilton."

"How did you know she'd come here?" I asked. "Did you follow her?"

"No," he answered. "My discovery that she'd come to see you was sheer accident—or maybe it was Fate. I'd read in the evening papers the preceding day how Fosdick, in what I assume was a clumsy attempt on his part to preserve Government secrecy, had entered my house the night before in the hope of finding my notes on the experiment we were conducting together. Realizing that he'd need them for the completion of his part of the work, and not wanting to take the chance in any case of their accidentally falling into the wrong hands—although heaven knows the experiment they concern isn't of sufficient importance to be ranked among our major defense secrets—I decided to slip back and get them for him myself at a time when I felt sure the policemen left on duty would be least expecting a visitor, and to send them to him anonymously through the mail.

"As I came up the street toward my house, I saw

Nora Hilton turn in at this one—I was able to recognize her from the picture of her the newspapers had printed when she was being sought in connection with Mark's alibi. I decided then that Fosdick and the notes would have to wait, that it was more important for me to learn what she had come to see you about.

"The French doors into this room were standing open, so I crept up onto the porch outside to overhear what I could. I heard her tell the first part of her story corroborating Mark's alibi, then say to you that there was something Barto had told her about Mark when he had first brought her here which she believed might have some bearing upon the murder; and I guessed immediately what it was."

He paused the barest instant, then added, "I had killed once to preserve that secret; it wasn't difficult for me to kill a second time. It never occurred to me until you pointed it out this evening that in destroying Nora Hilton, I had also destroyed Mark's alibi."

He ceased speaking, as though suddenly aware that he had reached the end of his story.

"It's odd," he observed after a moment in an entirely different tone, "how, once a man starts talking about a thing of this kind, he finds a queer relief in just going on until he's talked himself out. But I'd better leave now before your wife gets back." A faint suggestion of irony crept into his voice. "Sorry I can't stay and help you prove your case, Laing, but at least I've given you the satisfaction of knowing that your solution was the correct one." He took a step toward the screen doors through which he had entered.

"What about Mark?" I asked.

He stopped. "What about him?"

"You can't let him stand trial for the crimes you committed."

"Why not?" he retorted with a return to the cold cynicism which had characterized him when he had first come into the room. "Mark is no son of mine in any sense of the word. I lost him to his real father last Thursday night."

"That isn't true," I contradicted. "Since that evening, you've been letting what Barto said to you eat into your mind until it's festered there. But Barto lied to you. Mark proved that himself, first when he left the theater with you that night, and again later when he returned here voluntarily, grief-stricken because of your supposed death. But even if you refuse to believe that he is still your son in everything except birth, you cannot deny that you are still his father. You proved it by coming here this evening in the first place, and you proved it again and again in the course of what you've just been telling me. You can't turn your back on him when he needs your help."

"You're wrong," he denied, but I noticed that his voice lacked its former assurance. "Whatever I may have felt for Mark at one time is dead now."

"No, it is not dead," I retorted, "any more than your old love for Helena Stedman is dead. We do not stop loving, Fordyce, simply because we are no longer loved in return, even though we may deny that love to ourselves and call it by the name of its opposite, hate. If you don't act to save Mark now, if you permit him to be dragged through all the ignominy of a trial for murder, perhaps even to be sent to his death, because of an accident of birth which was no fault of his, all that you have suffered during the past twenty years will be as nothing to the living hell that the remainder of your life will become; for you will not only have sacrificed your son, you will have lost your wife all over again."

"Stop!" The word cut through mine like a cry of anguish. For the space of several seconds, there was no sound in the room save that of his labored breathing as he fought for control of himself. At last:

"You're right," he admitted, and his voice had once again become suddenly tired, as though the weight of the years had descended upon him. "I can't go through with it. I think I've realized from the beginning that I couldn't, although I tried to goad myself with the thing that I have allowed to poison my life for twenty years. But it's no use." He took a deep breath, then added quietly, "I'll go with you to the police, and give myself up."

CHAPTER XXV

We left the house together in silence. After we had walked a little over a block, Fordyce spoke.

"You've got to promise me one thing, Laing," he said abruptly. "Promise me you'll let me give the police my own explanation of why I killed Barto and Nora Hilton."

"What will it be?" I asked.

"That he came to the house and we quarreled over my refusal to let Mark take part in the play," he answered. "With a man of his excitable temperament, a quarrel of that kind could very easily have led to violence. Besides, everyone who was at the theater that night knows what a state of white-hot fury I was in when I came there.

"As for Miss Hilton," he paused uncertainly, as though that part of his solution had been more difficult to think out, "let us say I was afraid she'd recognized me on the street as she was coming to your house, and that I killed her to make sure of her silence. She couldn't have, of course, since we had never met; but only she and I knew that. The explanation would hold water, at least; and giving it instead of the right one wouldn't alter the essential facts of the case, but it would mean a lot to me—and to Mark."

I promised.

"Thank you," he said simply, and we went on again in silence.

Presently the rumble of cross-town traffic told me we were approaching the main thoroughfare, which we would have to cross in order to take the in-bound bus that would carry us to police headquarters. As we reached the curb, Fordyce put out his hand automatically to check my progress; but I had already heard the sound of the onrushing bus that was bound in the opposite direction, and stopped on my own accord.

Not so Fordyce. As though unaware of what he was doing, he stepped from the curb and straight into the path of the speeding bus.

There was the scream of tires as the driver frantically applied his brakes. But no man could have stopped his vehicle quickly enough at such short notice. . . .

Eric Fordyce died of his injuries that night at the university hospital, but not before he had regained consciousness long enough to recognize Mark, who had been released from custody in response to my telephone call to McDermott, and who remained at his father's bedside until the end came.

After it was all over, I gave McDermott the explanation of the two murders that I knew Fordyce had wanted me to give. The lieutenant accepted it and wrote it into the official record that closed the case; and if he suspected that there was more than I had told, he didn't betray the fact by asking questions. One of the things I have come to admire most about McDermott is his ability to recognize that there are certain occasions when it is unnecessary for the police to know everything.

Later I gave the same explanation to Mark, even embroidering it a little to suggest self-defense. Deirdre, who was present at the time, told me afterwards it was the most beautiful lie she had ever heard.

"But you know, Paddy," she confided, "I can't help wondering a little about how Dr. Fordyce was killed. It seems impossible that he shouldn't have seen or heard the bus coming."

I said nothing, remembering his hand upon my arm to prevent me from stepping off the curb.

"It was really best that it happened as it did," she went on after a little while, and I had the feeling that she had understood my silence. "This way, he's been spared all the torture of a public trial—and what must have come afterwards. Besides, there was always the chance that someone might have remembered his name, and dug up that old scandal. Now no one will ever know but us."

"And Prentiss," I amended, recalling his part in solving the mystery. "But don't worry, Derry: he'll never tell. For over twenty years ago, he, too, was more than half in love with Helena Stedman."